Sanitarium Magazine
Issue no. 22

Thank you to all of our contributors, we couldn't have done it without you.

Contents

ISSUE TWENTY-TWO

Dear Reader,

Welcome to the twenty-second issue of Sanitarium. In this issue we have nine great stories, 3 dark verse, a new section called the Hope Spot, a review from Nancy and an interview with Bobby Adair.

The horror community has had a difficult time of late with the slender-man issues, articles written about the poor equality of women portrayed in fiction – I am not going to add fuel to this fire

– it will burn itself out soon enough and we can continue on trying to scare the crap out of each other.

What I will say however is this, no matter what you write – keep writing. There is always an audience and people will always find a way to read your stories – we all like to be scared witless as we sit reading by candle or torchlight in the enveloping darkness.

We hope you enjoy the latest issue and if you leave a review or rate us – let us know, as we want to know what is working and what can be worked on.

Barry Skelhorn

Fishing Buddies

Seth Ojala

Physician: Dr. Roundtree
8245-AVD12

ALL FISHERMEN HAVE TOLD A TALL FISH TALE at some point in their life, and I have one, but I've never told my story until now. It's a fish tale of sorts that even I can hardly believe, but I do believe, for it happened to me. Today is October 12, 1995. My fish tale, my nightmare, happened on July 10, 1985.

My name is Jacob Arnold and I was born on March 2, 1935 on a cold and snowy spring evening to my parents Paul and Mary Arnold. My friend and eventual fishing buddy, Samuel Peerson, was born later the same year on a warm, summer evening. He was born on June 6, 1935.

Now, we both grew up in the small town of Harling, Michigan. We went to the same school. We were teammates on the Harling Howlers football team. He was a linebacker, and I was a wide receiver. Sammy and I did everything together. Those who didn't know us to thought we were brothers, for we even had the same color hair and were both tall and solidly built. We were popular and good looking and we knew it.

Sammy and I were not only friends, but we were fishing buddies. For those who don't know, a fishing buddy is the best kind of friend that a man could have. Now mind you, not just any kind of friend can be a fishing buddy. Only a certain kind of best friend can apply and be hired for the position of a fishing buddy. A good fishing buddy knows when to talk and when to shut up. A good fishing buddy brings enough beer to last the entire outing. Good old Sammy was the perfect candidate; he was the only candidate.

Fishermen usually always prefer a specific fishing hole, and we were no different. Ours was Cloud Lake just south of the Harling town border. We always talked about how great it would be to get married to a beautiful girl and then get a place right off the lake and live in peace and quiet. Life has its funny way of doing things, and Sammy's wish came true.

Sammy married his highschool sweetheart Marilyn Chase and then bought a small cabin on the edge of town at the end of a dead-end dirt road less than a quarter mile away from Cloud Lake. They loved their privacy. I married my highschool sweetheart, Charlene May, a year after him but we chose to live in town to be closer to Charlene's elderly parents. Every other weekend though we would visit Sammy and Marilyn out at their place though and play cards. Their lifestyle was much quieter and simple than ours, but there was an attractiveness to it. Charlene even mentioned moving out closer to them in our golden years, and I was in total agreement. The closer to Sammy we lived the more fishing he and I could fit into our busy lives, but even amongst the hecticness that is life Sammy and I still managed to get plenty of fishing in.

For years we fished together. We fished all over the state of Michigan, but our favorite fishing hole was still right outside of Harling on Cloud Lake. Cloud lake was only about fifty acres from one shore to the next, but it was sufficient for a couple of lazy fishermen like us.

The lake was well protected from the wind. Tall, thick trees grew seemingly on every spare inch of shore line, and it was because of the lack of shore line that made Cloud Lake hard to access. An unaccessible lake helped make it a quiet lake. It was a tranquil, peaceful fishing hole, and it was all ours. Sammy really enjoyed it too because it was so close to home for him. He had even blazed himself a nice trail that went through the woods and emptied out into his backyard. It was a bit of a hike, but it was an easy, pleasant hike. I would always drive to his place and then together we would walk the trail down to the lake.

Cloud lake teemed with all kinds of fish too. Panfish of all sorts, bass, northern pikes, musky, perch, and even some walleye all inhabited Cloud Lake's waters. Our humble sailing vessel was a fourteen-foot aluminum boat named Betsy, named after Sam's sister, who had died at the age of six from pneumonia. For years as we were growing up, Sam and I ventured onto the stilled waters of Cloud Lake in Betsy to haul in a day's catch. As we grew older, our ventures slowed down a bit due to the typical adult responsibilities that eventually plague everyone, but we still managed to get out onto Cloud Lake's beckoning waters every other weekend.

Years passed and Sammy would lose Marilyn in 1980 to breast cancer. Sammy went into a depression for that first year without Marilyn, but in the summer of '81, he finally snapped out of it and we were out fishing again almost every weekend.

Our lifestyle continued this way until 1985, where my fish tale, the one I have kept secret for so long, really begins. Let me begin by telling you what kind of fishermen we were, for you see, it is crucial to the story.

I was a lure fisherman. I used fake worms and fake frogs. I used worms now and again, but I loved the fake lures. Anything that popped or rattled, I would tie it to my line. I loved the constant action and movement. I even had a good luck charm. A rabbit's foot that had been dyed blue hung around my neck at all times. Later as I got older, I just kept it in my pocket.

Sammy, on the other hand, only used bobbers and hooks. Unlike myself, he didn't need or strive for the constant movement and action. Sammy could just kick back, relax, and watch a bobber for hours without even moving it from its original casting point. Sometimes he would switch the color of the bobber from red and white to a yellow and brown pencil bobber, but at the end of the day he would only fish with a hook, worm and a bobber.

Sammy had a good luck charm too; one he wore around his neck. It was a gold colored, metal compass tied to a silver chain. The compass had been given to him by his sister Betsy the year before she had died. It was all he had left of her. He had it tied to a piece of polyester rope and wore it around his neck seven days a week. Inside the compass, hidden inside the latch compartment, was a picture of his sister Betsy that was taken the year she had died.

"Why don't you put that compass on a chain or something, Sammy?" I asked him one time.

"Polyester is much stronger than any rinky-dinky chain, Jacob. This compass will never fall off my neck." Sammy explained to me.

It didn't look very fashionable, but it was very practical I suppose.

It was on July 10 then, 1985, that it all happened. We were both fifty years old now, but our old age wasn't going to keep us from fishing. The day had started off a little breezy and warm, but when we got out onto the lake the wind had been blocked right out by our tall and trustworthy trees. We rowed Betsy out toward the middle of the lake, and even though we never had taken any accurate measurements, we figured that we were sitting in thirty-five to forty feet of water. Even though we had one we would not throw out the anchor, but rather slowly drift toward one shoreline or the other.

I started off with a green and blue jitterbug. Sammy started off with a white and red bobber. He cast sixty feet out and landed his bobber right in between two lily pads less than a foot apart from each other.

"How do you do it, Sammy?" I inquired of him as I always did when he would cast with such accuracy.

"That's how us pros do it, Jacob. All in the wrists." He replied simply.

The sun had come out to play and was warming things up nicely. The low morning fog over Cloud Lake had dispersed and left only a blue, empty canvas of beautiful sky. I was maneuvering my jitterbug beautifully across the still waters of our private little pond while Sammy sat and stared quietly at his still bobber.

Then it happened.

Sammy's red and white bobber popped, then it popped again. It popped four more times before it went down for good and that was when Sammy went into action. He set the hook and started to reel in, but it was of no use! Instead of the line coming into the reel the line started going out! The drag on his reel started to scream.

"Holy cow, Jacob! Musky!" Sammy excitedly yelped. I reeled in my jitterbug quickly as I continued to watch my old friend fight to reel in line, but whatever was on his hook was taking the line faster than he could reel it in. The only thing that could be taking line like that could only be a fierce, snarl-toothed, musky.

"Careful, Sammy, don't want to break the line, gonna have to wear it out." I coached, but we both knew what he had to do. Then the boat started to move. The monster at the other end of Sammy's line was actually pulling the boat!

"God, Jacob! She's moving us! By God, she's pulling the boat!" Sammy started laughing nervously.

"That ain't no she, Sammy, it's . . . it's gonna sink us! Cut the line!" I panicked. . Something wasn't right. Suddenly a foul smell pierced the air suddenly and it seemed to be originating from the bottom of the lake; the vile odor started to turn my stomach. It reeked of spoiled milk poured over day old road kill.

"Cut the line, Sammy!" I yelled again, but I knew from the look in his eyes that he had every intention of landing this monster fish that had now dragged Betsy forty feet from our original position. The bobber was now deep enough under the water that we could no longer see it. Whatever was on the other end of his line was going away from the boat toward the shoreline.

I dropped my rod and was going to help when the unimaginable happened. What occurred next still gives me sweat drenching nightmares to this day, because it was the moment that changed us forever. Sammy stood up to brace himself for the long fight when the monster on the other end of the line jerked violently throwing Sammy off balance and over the edge of the boat! I reached over quickly to try and grab the back of his T-shirt, but I wasn't quick enough and watched helplessly as he went head first into the dark waters of Cloud Lake.

Sammy, being the devout fisherman that he was, kept hold of his rod even though he was now treading water. I watched as he kept trying (unsuccessfully) to reel in the monster. He was a madman possessed!

"Let go!" I screamed, but it was of no use. Sammy held onto his rod with dear life and I watched helplessly as he was dragged across the top of the water for fifty or so feet like a fallen skier being dragged atop the water by a jet boat. Suddenly he was pulled under the dark surface of the water and was gone. I had never seen or imagined that any fish besides a shark or a whale could have ever moved with such speed and velocity. No, something unnatural was doing this, and it made my very bones quake in terror.

I was in a full cold panic now and didn't know what to do at first. I was frozen for only a moment but it felt like hours before I finally snapped out of my trance and snatched up the oars to Betsy. I started for the spot where I had seen Sammy go down.

"Sammy! SAMMY! Where are you?" I screamed as I rowed maniacally, but I heard nothing in reply. Besides my panicked rowing, Cloud Lake was eerily silent. One moment he was there, and then in an instant he was just gone. I started to cry. I started to leave my body in a strange out-of-body way. I was paralyzed with fear and could feel myself going into shock.

Just when I started to despair, I heard a splash. I looked around frantically for the source of the disturbance. Another splash! This time it was behind me. I turned around to see Sammy! He was splashing around in a very frenzied manner. I rowed over to him as fast as I could and when I did, I reached over to help him back into the boat, trying carefully not to tip the boat over and put us both back into the drink. When I finally got Sammy back safely into the boat, I noticed that his face was ghostly white and he looked very ill. "Good Lord, Sammy! What happened? That was insane! Why didn't you drop your rod?" I chastised. "Are you all right? You don't look so well." I was already starting back to shore, for I was done fishing for the day and I was quite sure that Sammy would have agreed if I had bothered asking. He didn't say a single word until we got back to shore.

"Let me help put Betsy up on her side and then I'm going home, Jacob. I don't believe I will be fishing anytime soon." Sammy finally spoke.

"It could have been much worse, Sammy. At least you didn't lose your tackle box or your lucky compass!" I pointed to his chest toward the compass that had indeed survived his impromptu diving venture.

"Yes, very true. See you later, Jacob." Sammy said simply and without any emotion. He turned and walked off quickly up the trail through the woods leading back to his house without saying another word to me. I put the rest of my things in order and walked the trail back to Sammy's by myself recalling everything that had just happened. When I got to his backyard, I saw that he had already shut the lights out inside his house. I shrugged and got into my car and simply drove away. We would never fish together again after that day.

A lot of questions remained unanswered after Sammy's fall into the lake. What was it that lay beneath the waters of Cloud Lake that had taken us for such a violent ride that day? What had pulled Sammy under the water like that? I had called him frequently afterwards to see how he was doing and if he wanted to go back out fishing, maybe out to a different lake even, but he refused me every time. In fact, every time he did answer the phone, he seemed. . . foreign. Foreign and distant would be the best way to put it I suppose.

Now most fish tales would have ended right here, but this is where my fish tale to beat all fish tales really starts getting interesting. It was soon after Sammy's impromptu fall into Cloud Lake, you see, that the Butcher's killings began.

It had been three weeks since our adventure on Cloud Lake when the first murder happened. The murder itself rocked our small town, but it was believed to be isolated, until the second murder, and then the third, and then the fourth. Soon, small town Harling had gone national with the headline: SERIAL KILLER TERRORIZES NORTHERN MICHIGAN!

By the end of August there were twelve murders, three males and nine females. Six of those nine females were between the ages of sixteen and nineteen years old. The three males that were killed ranged in age between twenty and thirty years of age. The victims were all also taken in their sleep. Messages left at the crime scene written in blood and entrails were left behind to taunt the police. One such message was leaked to the media by a spotlight hungry deputy and it said simply: MEAT IS GREAT.

Everyone in Harling was on guard and on high alert that summer. Nobody dared go anywhere without some kind of company. Everyone, including myself and Charlene, slept with the lights on and the doors barricaded. The media had given the killer the nickname the Butcher, which I despised, but the media will do what they do best, and that is to try to make everything into a Hollywood special.

During the summer of the Butcher, I had continued trying to keep in touch with Sammy, but eventually I just kind of gave up. He had become a recluse again like he had done before just after Marilyn had passed. I went out fishing two other times by myself that summer, but both times I was a nervous wreck, for I was terrified that whatever had bit Sammy's hook that day would try and bite mine! Both times I went out I was sure to have a sharp knife with me to cut the line in a hurry if need be. I was also concerned, of course, about the Butcher. I kept a constant eye on the tree line surrounding Cloud Lake half expecting the mad Butcher to be hiding behind a tree just waiting for me to come back to shore for a tasty snack. My first solo trip out was uneventful, but it was the second time I went out by myself that something very peculiar happened.

I was rowing back to shore with a modest day's catch when I spotted Sammy standing on the shore with his hands in his pockets. When I first saw him, he startled me, for I hardly recognized my old friend. His face was ghostly white and he had lost a lot of hair since I had seen him last. He wore an ugly, green turtleneck which I found strange being he had always despised turtlenecks. His lips
were almost blue and his eyes seemed foggy. I gave him a nervous wave. He didn't return my wave; he just stared at me. The look on his face mortified me.

"Hello, Jacob." Sammy spoke finally when I arrived to shore. "Sammy, how are you? You feeling OK? You want to go out fishing?" I asked. "I was just coming back in, but I'm willing to go back out!"

"No, no. Just wanted to ask you something." He seemed . . . off. "Ask away, buddy. Sure, good to see you. Starting to get worried about you. Don't see much of you at all these days." I hopped out of Betsy and Sammy helped me drag her up and out of the water.

"That's what I wanted to ask you. Have people been talking about me? You know, about me not coming around and being . . reclusive?" He looked at me, and that was when I saw something hiccup underneath his right ear beneath his turtleneck shirt. I backed away instantly on instinct, and Sammy caught whiff of my fear. "Why, Jacob? You act like you've seen a ghost! It's just a neck spasm! It started after my dip into the lake that day and it's gotten worse. I should go see a doctor, but you know how I hate hospitals. It's just a neck spasm, buddy. It's weird and that's why I wear this awful shirt. So, has anyone been asking questions?"

I was still nervous, but at the time I wanted to believe his story about neck spasms, for my mind was beginning to run away with all sorts of unimaginable horrors. "Well, you need to go see a doctor, Jacob. You don't look well at all." My nerves and my heartbeat were slowing down a little bit, but not enough. "But the answer to your question is no. Nobody is asking questions. Why, what's going on, man? I think you need to get those . . . spasms looked at, man."

"Bah . . . it's nothing. I was just wondering. Just curious is all. With all this Butcher stuff going on I don't want people start pointing fingers my way. I know that I am quite the recluse now and all. I can't explain it, Jacob, but that's just how it is now. Goodbye." He turned around abruptly and ran off funny into the woods.

When I say funny, I mean that he ran stiff armed and awkwardly as if he had forgotten how to run altogether. When he ran it looked as if someone had tied his arms to his side and lit the back of his pants on fire! It sounds funny, but I assure you, it was not funny.

In fact, it was not as much humorous as it was terrifying and it left me standing cold and numb besides Cloud Lake. Something was wrong with Sammy, and I had every intention of finding out what was wrong with him. Perhaps he had suffered brain damage when he had fallen into the lake, and without medical attention, Sammy could be in mortal danger.

I immediately went home and told Charlene who agreed with me about possible brain damage, especially after I told her and demonstrated to her Sammy's funny run. At first, she started to laugh, but then she too became very concerned and sincerely troubled when she stopped to think about it.

"You need to go to town and get Dr. Williamson. Take him to see Sammy right now. You have to help him, Jacob." Charlene was right and so I did. I went right to town and got Dr. Williamson and told him about Sammy.

It took some convincing, but after a moment's consideration he called his wife to cancel dinner plans for that evening and then together we rode in my car out to Sammy's house. In a small town like Harling where everybody knows your name, we take care of our own. We had started up the driveway when we spotted Sammy darting frantically across his backyard and into his house through the back door. Dr. Williamson witnessed first hand his strange, armless, running style.

"Let's see what has happened to the poor boy. I do believe you are right in thinking he may have suffered some minor brain damage, Jacob." We got out of my car and made our way up to the front door and knocked. I was about to yell out Sammy's name when I heard a woman scream. Dr. Williamson and I both were both startled by the blood curdling scream and I immediately went to open the door, but it was locked.

"Sammy! Sammy! What's going on in there?" I yelled out.

"Stand back, Jacob." I moved aside and watched as Dr. Williamson proceeded to kick the door in. The door flew off the jamb with his second kick. "I've always wanted to do that." He said with a smirk.

We ran into Sammy's home. The door that doc had kicked in led into his living room. The woman screamed again from somewhere in the back of the house. Having been in Sammy's home so many times before I knew that the screams were coming from the kitchen.

We dashed through the living room, through the dining room and emptied into the kitchen where we saw a naked girl tied to one of Sammy's sturdy oak chairs from his dining room. The girl was bleeding from head to toe and it took a second before I recognized her; the girl was Shelly Marks, a cashier from the Shop-&-Go in town.

She was crying and when she saw us she started shrieking loudly. Doc and I went to her and started to untie her but she kept shrieking. Her breathing was labored and she was choking on her own spit. I tried to comfort her, but was having no such luck. Doc started to help me untie her.

"Shelly! Calm down, dear. We aren't going to hurt you. Where's Sammy? Did he do this to you?" I asked her. How could Sammy do something like this? I wondered to myself.

As I was asking myself this when Shelly suddenly screamed, "Watch OUT!" Out of the corner of my left eye I saw Doc fall to the ground like a ton of bricks. I went to turn around, but it was too late. I heard what sounded like an iceberg splitting from its glacier going off inside my head. My whole world went black.

I was immobile for what must have been a few hours. I recall going in and out of consciousness while I was laid out on Sammy's kitchen floor, and I saw things that were so awful that to this day I still scream myself awake when these memories visit me in the middle of the night.

I saw Sammy with sharp claws at the end of his fingers. Pink, bloody gills pulsating wildly from the sides of Sammy's neck. Then I watched as Sammy unhinged his lower jaw out of place like an anaconda and started to engulf Doc's legs, and then his torso. Then he started feasting upon Shelly. Sammy's dark, beady eyes watched me as he dined feverishly. I was looking upon a creature from Hell itself! I could hear his teeth cutting on bone and innards being crushed as they passed slowly down his now grotesquely extended throat. I passed out again and awoke several hours later. I was still on the kitchen floor. I looked around and was horrified at what I saw. There was little left of Shelly Marks. All that was left of her were her two legs and a pile of guts. Docs' severed head was resting in between her feet. The rest of Doc was gone. Placed at my feet was a hastily written note taped to the same brick that Sammy
had brought down onto the back of my skull.

Jacob,

Meat is good. Fishing is good. I'm leaving now. Need new meat. I wouldn't bother telling the police what you saw. They won't believe you.
Yours truly,

The Butcher ;)
PS. If you ever come to San Jose . . . look me up.

Sammy, my friend, the Butcher, wasn't human. I had come face to face with a monster and it had let me live. The police wouldn't believe what I saw, Sammy was right, but I still had to call the police. I decided to leave the details of what I had seen to myself though. I also didn't bother showing them the letter either.

Later the police would piece together some kind of story about how the Butcher had killed Doc, Shelly and presumably Sammy as well, although they had never found Sammy's body, and I knew they wouldn't. Not unless they were planning a trip to San Jose. Sammy was the Butcher, and he was also some kind of inhuman monster. I still couldn't believe it. I still try telling myself to this day that what I saw in the kitchen that day was nothing but an awful dream, but it wasn't. It all happened.

I wish this was the end of my terrible fish tale, but what good fish tale doesn't have a little twist at the ending?

It was a few weeks later that I decided to go fishing again. I went to Cloud Lake and rowed out to the middle of the lake at about the same spot that Sammy had fell in that fateful day and threw the anchor out and just sat there. I sat there for about two hours or so just thinking about things before I finally decided to pull up my anchor and row back to shore. I started to tug on the anchor rope when suddenly I felt it snag onto something. It was something heavy.

I yanked with all my might and slowly the anchor started to come up. I thought that I must have snagged a tree limb or something, but as the anchor drew closer to the surface I saw something that made me scream out in horror. It was Sammy! Sammy's decomposing, rotting flesh of a corpse! His polyester rope and compass had become wrapped around my anchor and now Sammy was staring up at me under the water with empty eye sockets. The many inhabitants of the lake had eaten them away. Black, hideous leeches were sucking away at what little was remaining of his face. I wanted to drop the anchor right away, but I had to be sure so I reached down into the cold water and reached for the compass and snapped it open. Inside was a picture of his sister Betsy.

I grabbed my knife with my free hand and cut the strong polyester rope tied to his compass from around Sammy's neck and then I watched as his cadaver sunk slowly back to the bottom of the lake. I put the compass in my pocket, threw the anchor in the boat, and rowed back to shore as fast as I could.

Sammy, the human Sammy, had never resurfaced that fateful day. The real Sammy was rotting away at the bottom of Cloud Lake. Who, or what, had I pulled back into the boat that day then? My mind swam with questions, but I had no answers. All I had was a compass tied to a polyester rope.

After that day I decided two things. I was never going to San Jose and I would never fish again, for I am terrified of what lies beneath unknown waters. I know now that evil things murk there, and besides . . . fishing is no fun without a good fishing buddy.

The End

Case #26376
Seth Ojala

Details not released
at this time.

CLAYTON HILL SANITARIUM

Number 99

Daniel J Bickley

Physician: Dr. Peterson
8268-WCT29

THEY JUST CALLED NUMBER 96. That means they're just three away from me now. They're getting so close that I can hear their footsteps coming down the hall. I can hear them open the creaky, heavy metal door to 96's room. And now I can hear him struggling and screaming as they drag him away. It's hard to believe that that's going to be me soon.

It's silent now. They've taken him out of my earshot. Before, when the voices still talked to me in my head, I didn't think any noise could be worse than that. They shouted at me so loud that it became so hard to hear anything else. They told me what a useless, pathetic person I was, and how I'd be better off just slitting my wrists than continuing my worthless existence. But now I know I was wrong. Hearing them drag off number 96 as he struggled, knowing it's just a matter of time until the same happens to me, is far worse than anything the voices could ever say to me. Even now my hands are starting to shake more as I think of it, making it hard to write this.

I don't know how long I've been down here. I imagine that it's been days, but I have no way to know for sure. It feels like forever since I've seen the bright, radiant light of the sun. The longer I sit here in this stone cell, the lone fluorescent bulb in the corner giving off a thin, flickering light it gets harder and harder to accept that sunlight still exists. It's even stranger to think that I was once one of those blessed beings to feel the warm rays on my skin.

They just called number 97! Why didn't 96 last longer? I don't know what they're doing differently now, but they're going through us faster than ever.

I don't know why they put me down here. After I was brought to this institution, I tried so hard to be good. I did everything they asked. I tried to be friendly to all the nurses and the orderlies. I always took the pills they gave me no matter how bad the medicine made me feel. I always ate all my food even when it was a struggle to choke it down. I didn't even spread, listen to, or believe the tales people told about morbid experiments in the sub-basement, or the patients that disappeared without a trace. I did everything I could to be good.

I don't know what I did to anger them, but they finally decided to take me. They gave me a strange, huge blue pill one night that I'd never seen before. Of course, I took it. I didn't even ask a question about it. Then, just a second later, my head started spinning. My vision became blurry and my hearing became less defined, almost like I was underwater. Then I fell unconscious. When I came to I was here. The only clues as to where they took me were the stone walls, the lack of sunlight, and the number 99 painted above my door. All that wasn't much, but it was enough to tell me that I was in the sub-basement.

They just called 98! At least 97 lasted longer than 96. It won't be long before they come for me now.

The first thing I heard when I woke up in this dungeon was someone calling a number over a loudspeaker. It was 32. It took them a lot longer to go through those earlier numbers. It seemed like forever before they finally called for 33, and in the meantime there was just silence.

Back then I thought the silence was unnerving. It was absolute, deafening. It was so deafening that that I actually started wondering if I'd lost the ability to hear. I wondered, that is, until I heard the clear sound of a cart rolling down the hallway. It sounded heavy, and the wheels were squeaking as it moved towards my cell.

I don't entirely know why I did what I did next. Maybe I just wanted to see another human so I could feel like I wasn't alone in the world. Maybe I just wanted to see something other than the stone walls and dirt floor of my cell. It doesn't really matter though. What does is that I ran to the door and peered out the tiny, barred window at the hallway outside, waiting for the cart to pass. The light was even dimmer our there than it was in my cell, making it hard to see, but finally my eyes adjusted and revealed a completely new horror to me. I saw so much that I lamented the fact that I hadn't gone blind long before.

I saw a man pushing the cart, a huge, hulking, monster of a man. He was wearing a medical gown and gloves with red, yellow, and brown stains on them. His mouth was covered with a mask, though something about his eyes and cheeks told me that he was smiling underneath. The one mercy I received in that moment was that I wasn't able to see his horrific smile. That mercy was short lived, though, because then my attention turned to the cart.

It took me a second to recognize what the mass of flesh was, but then I realized that the cart was heaped with dead bodies. Their limp limbs were flopping out of the cart, brushing against the walls and the floor. Their glassy, dead eyes were still open, reflecting the dim light of the hallway with a morbid glare.

I ran away from the window in horror, retreating back into the far corner of my cell, trying to keep myself from puking. That was the first clue I got about what they were doing to us patients. I wish I could say that it was the last, but it wasn't. There have been two more carts since then, each worse than the last. I don't know why I kept getting up to see them pass, but I did.

On the second cart I saw there were severed hands, feet, legs, arms, and heads. There wasn't a single torso in sight. Blood was dripping onto the ground, leaving a trail of dead fluids in the cart's wake. I nearly fainted when I saw that cart. My legs went weak, like jelly, and I collapsed to the floor with my back resting against the door, my heart feeling like it was going to beat out of my chest. I couldn't imagine that anything worse could be possible. I had no idea how wrong I was.

The third and last cart I saw was by far the worst for me, even if it wasn't as gory as the others. For on that last cart there were people, living people, piled one on top of another. Their mouths were hanging open dumbly, saliva dripping down their chins. I thought the glares of the corpses' eyes were bad, but theirs were far worse. Their glassy and dilated eyes darted here and there as the cart moved until one of their gazes even met my own. That woman looked into my eyes almost pleadingly as tears began to fall down her cheeks. That was the moment when I finally did faint out of horror. Even now just thinking about it is making my stomach turn, and my head get lighter.

Oh no! They just called my number! They called number 99!

I can hear them approaching my cell now! They're almost here! I hope they don't find this. Who knows what they'll do to me if they see this?

They're opening the door now! Dear God, please help my soul. And may he help yours if you're reading this.

The End.

Case #96843
Daniel J Bickley

Daniel J. Bickley was born in Sandusky, Ohio in September of 1991. In the third grade he read The Hobbit and The Lord Of The Rings for the first time. Those works filled his mind and fueled his imagination until his freshman year of high school, when he first fell in love with writing and storytelling.

Ever since then he hasn't stopped working to develop his individual style and voice in the hopes of making a career out of his passion. He's currently trying to get more short stories and poems published and is working on finishing a novel entitled Through The Shadow Of Death. His favorite writers are Alexandre Dumas, H.P. Lovecraft, and J.R.R. Tolkien.

CLAYTON HILL SANITARIUM

Feast Your Eyes

Cindy Morren

KATO'S CRY COULD TURN DREAMS INTO NIGHTMARES. The mere shrill of his howl gave me goosebumps in my sleep, and was more than enough to wake me up. I looked at the clock noticing it had stopped at 2:05 am. I wasn't sure when it happened, but had thought before bed it was fine. My brief curiosity of time however was interrupted by Kato's howling. I only heard him howl one other time in my life. One night a few years back, I had lost my footing and slipped down the stairs, breaking my arm and fracturing my jaw. I lay there, still as a rock, and Kato hearing the commotion saw me there lifeless. His bark sent a jolt through my body, piercing my muddy thoughts.

I got up and put my slippers on, trying to sift through the blue-black darkness. I was breathing heavily, feeling as though my muscles ached from a soreness I could not quite understand. Yesterday I had done nothing to develop fatigue, and I usually slept soundly. I could feel the tightness of my muscles with each move, and started to massage the nape of my neck as I felt an ache there too. Approaching the stairs, I walked down slowly trying to wake my body up, and then I heard it; the piercing silence. Kato's howling was interrupted by something, as if he had seen someone.

"Kato?" I said shakily.

The house got colder, in a way that wasn't the November weather, but something else-- something sinister. I finally reached the bottom of the staircase to see Kato backing away slowly from the window, the only sound in the room were his paws against the cold hardwood floor. I watched him for a moment noticing he was trembling.

My eyes inched up from his body towards the window slowly and carefully. Before I could scream, the face put its finger against its lips in a "shhh" motion. I stared at what appeared to be something that couldn't be real. Its teeth were decayed, gums completely black. Its face was deteriorating, rotting even. But the eyes are what scared me the most. It had no eyes. Just black spaces where eyes had once been, appearing as though they had been ripped out. The air got colder, and I could see my breath escape my lips. The figure smiled at me, this wide grin that was almost threatening as it was mocking. It was taunting me, realizing my fear. Its head turned in almost a snapping motion to the side, the bones in its neck making a loud harsh cracking sound. It walked past my door slowly until its silhouette reached the biggest window in my living room. It stopped there, turned its body and breathed heavily against the glass. Arching its head back, it banged its head incessantly against the window, cracking it slightly until it broke into pieces, glass shattering everywhere.

Just as I was focused on the figure in the living room, it disappeared in an instant. The front door slammed open breaking the sudden silence in the room, but no one was standing there. Before I could grab him, Kato ran out, trying to protect us both.

"Kato, NO!"I cried, tears streaming down my face.

I went to follow him, but stopped at the door as I heard him shriek somewhere in the night beyond the trees. Something had Kato, something killed him. And it was coming for me. I shut the door, locked it, and ran as fast as I could. I ran up the spiral staircase, my heartbeat pounding in my chest, deafening the sound of my loud footsteps. A loud creak on the steps paralyzed me against my own will. I turned hesitantly, seeing the figure at the very bottom of the stairs with the same evil grin it had at the window. It was on its hands and knees crawling up towards me, its bones cracking as it did before. I ran again, finally reaching the top, hearing the figure inch closer. As I got into my room, I slammed the door shut just as the figure reached the top of the stairs. As I closed the door, it turned to me pausing at the top, and I noticed its hair was bloody and it wore a nightgown. It was a woman, and even though its face was without eyes, I felt as though I knew her.

I got into bed, not knowing what else to do, terrified of moving or making a sound. The heavy silence was back again with the bitter cold. I laid in bed trembling; knowing my only way out was through the front door. I went back to my bedroom door, opening it slightly seeing no sight of the eyeless woman. As I closed it quietly, I wiped the tears from my face, but I didn't turn around. I couldn't. My heart was pounding again in my chest, and the air was colder than ever, except the steady heat of breath on my neck. I peered into the mirror on my door seeing the figure behind me, next to my bed. I turned quickly but she disappeared again. I turned again towards the mirror and saw her standing there staring back at me. Not behind me, not next to me. The figure was me. I let out a terrified cry, even though the sightless image of me was smiling. My door sprang open, Kato appearing just beyond it. It didn't make sense. He came towards me, dropping what appeared to be the remnants of eyes.

Then I knew. The night I had fallen was no accident. I never slipped and lost my footing, I killed myself. Kato had discovered me there - jaw, arm and neck broken instantly from the fall. It took weeks for someone to discover that I was dead, that my body lay decaying in my house. When they had finally arrived, Kato chewed on what was left of my eyes, blood drops escaping his lips. The clock pounded at 2:05 am, my time of death. Having no family or close friends, I was alone both in the physical world and now in the spiritual. Caught in the hell of limbo for my suicide, I sat back in my chair staring at the dark space inside me.

The End

Case #46311

Cindy Morren

Cindy Morren lives in New York where she studies English and minors in Psychology. When she is not being studious, she enjoys writing anything that comes to her dark and exquisitely sinister mind.

The Worm out of Space

Jonathan Anderson

THEY WERE VERY FAR AWAY FROM HOME.

At night in the dark, their mother told them bedtime stories about the world they had left long ago. She told them that they would be returning soon. She told them that they were important and special. She told them of faraway and lofty things. But when she said goodnight and them alone, Quinn told the stories about their here and now.

"Way out here," said Quinn one night, "there is a gigantic worm. His name is Wyxyr. He eats people if they get too close to where he lives. People don't know exactly where he lives, so they can't avoid him. That's how he stays alive. The worm's tail is tied in a gigantic knot, and the worm goes on forever inside of the knot. He can eat as many people as there are in the whole universe."

Samuel's eyes drifted along the steel frame of the bed above him supporting the bunk where Quinn lay, invisible to his eyes. "You know what happens to you outside?"

"No," said Samuel, making his answer sound as final as he could, hoping to end this night's particular story.

"First, you scream," said Quinn. He let the words linger in the dead air and then continued. "At least, you should try to scream. You would want to squeeze all of the air out of your lungs, or else your body would explode. You would want to close your eyes too, otherwise they would freeze and dry out and you would never be able to use them again."

"It's cold in space, I know," said Samuel.

"It's very cold. It's colder than the coldest night ever was back home. You would turn into ice. You would turn into ice starting with your mouth and your nose. Dad told me about it yesterday in science."

"You turn into ice?"

"Yeah, but not for a while. If you are out there long enough your skin turns blue and you turn into ice."

Samuel rolled over in his cot.

"That is," Quinn said, "unless the worm eats you first." Samuel shut his eyes tight. Quinn breathed a laugh through his nose, and then all was quiet.

Samuel lay awake a long time before sleep took him.

***

He woke in a sweat, his mind racing with images of frozen bodies and the terrible worm from space. He got out of bed and darted through the bedroom door. He went across the hall to where his parents slept.

He climbed into bed on his mother's side. Sleepily, his mother lifted the heavy, warm blankets and made room for his small body. "Quinn tells such scary stories," Samuel said, burying his face into his mother's chest. "That terrible monster, and all of those dead people. It can't be true, can it?"

"No," said his mother. Her eyes were looking away from him. It can't be true, she told him. Or perhaps she was just thinking to herself. It was difficult to tell sometimes.

***

Their living space constituted only a small portion of their saucer-shaped craft. Their quarters formed the center, a two-story cylinder. Surrounding the cylinder, in the gently narrowing outer circle of the craft was room for agriculture, the downward-sloping ceiling lined with imitation-solar lights. Mother and Father tended the crops and harvested fresh food for them to eat. Underneath the floor of all these spaces were the gravity units and the battery, charged continuously by the family's waste.

On this particular morning (which for them meant that the lights of their living quarters gradually brightened, and recorded music played at increasing volume over a system of speakers), Mother returned early from the garden with fresh fruit for breakfast.

The boys ate oranges and strawberries while their father led their morning discussion as he always did. Their father had a large, circular scar on his forehead above his left eye, like a crater in his skin, that Samuel would stare at when his mind wandered. During these morning talks, Father offered the boys encouragement, or addressed their growing morality.

"Remember, it's important to believe in yourself," he said to them. "Nothing is more important than your success. If you only believe in yourself, you can achieve anything."

Quinn always looked at his father with bright eyes, sometimes nodding as he listened to him speaking. Samuel never quite understood what his father meant, but assumed that he would when he got to be as old as Quinn.

Their father took a breath but before he could speak again, a dull thud resounded in the cabin.

Instinctively, they looked up even though it was clear that the noise had come from outside of the room, possibly outside of the ship itself.

Father stood up, still looking at the ceiling in the direction of the noise.

They heard another thud. This time, it came from the side of the ship, in the direction of the terrarium.

Father got up and walked away from the table. The boys remained quiet, listening. Father climbed the ladder into the room above the kitchen where the navigation equipment was. Quinn got up from his chair and followed him. Samuel stuffed a slice of orange into his mouth and then followed Quinn.

The navigation room was dark, lit only by the light from the control panel spread out before Father, whom the boys saw as a dark silhouette against the electronic display. Father touched a button and a sliding aperture opened to reveal a window spanning the dome-shaped ceiling of the room.

As the aperture slid open, they saw something float past just outside the window, moving out of sight before they could make out what it was.

Their father stood up and motioned to his boys to stay still. They waited in silence, watching the motionless expanse of stars above.

Suddenly, there was another thud--louder this time-- followed by a slow, soft brushing sound. Whatever had run into the hull of their ship was sliding toward them, toward the window.

Through the cockpit window they saw the dark form of a man, head appearing first, then shoulders, then body. Father pressed the button on the console for the cockpit lights. A ring of lights rimming the circular room flooded on, illuminating the white-gray walls, finally falling on the person in the window.

In the light, they could see that it was a dead man--face bloated and blue, eyes obscured by crusty frost.

Then, with the soft brushing sound, the body slid out of sight. Father touched several buttons on the console now, and the ship pitched downward. Looking through the upper window, the boys and their father saw dozens more frozen, blue bodies, drifting toward them in the silent vastness.

"Go back down," Father said.

The boys didn't move.

"Go down," Father repeated. Quinn, with a subtle expression of shame, turned and descended the ladder. Samuel did the same.

***

They sat in silence together for a long time after that. The fruit did not seem appealing, and they ate little more. Samuel kept expecting Quinn to say something, but he never did. Then he figured that it must be Father who should say the next thing and that they were waiting for him.

"Dad," Quinn finally said, "were those real?"

"Yes, son," his father said, eyes fixed sullenly on the white table before them.

"I didn't think they would look like that," Quinn said. "I had a dream about them after you told me, and they looked just like that. I didn't think they were real though, when I woke up. I thought, 'They can't really look like that.'"
Father turned to look at him, his eyes as fixed as the stars.
"You say you've seen this before?" said Father.
"Yes," said Quinn. "I dreamt it before, after you told me about it in science."
"That was two days ago," said Father to himself. "Enough time to..."
Samuel said, "I had a dream about it last night." "Yeah, after I told you about it, dummy," Quinn spat.
Father put out his hand and said, "Quinn was speaking to me, Samuel; please let him finish."
Samuel crossed his arms and put his chin down behind them so that his nose rested just above his elbows.
"They look just like your dream?" said Father.
"Yes," said Quinn.
Mine, too, thought Samuel.
Father slowly turned his head to look at Mother, who had been sitting at the table, motionless.
"This is the time," Father said to her.
Her face was pale, but her eyes were hard as stone. She nodded.
"Time for what?" said Quinn.
Father breathed deeply and put his hands on the table. The boys could tell that he was about to say something very important.
"There is something that you don't know yet," their father said. "But I think that you are old enough to know. Our family has gift--a very special, rare gift--that goes back very far in our family. It's the reason we're here, instead of back home, on Earth.

"Your grandfather, Aldous, was a magician. He was what people call a 'Maker.' There have only been two or three of them in the history of mankind. As a Maker, your grandfather had the power, by thinking long and hard enough about one thing, to make it into something real, even if it wasn't real to begin with."

Quinn's eyes glowed.

"It was an awesome power," Father continued, "and with it, he made all sorts of things, like tools and weapons. But one night, he had a terrible nightmare. It was so intense that it took hold of his entire mind, and it made the terrible thing in his nightmare. That thing was fire."

Quinn's eyes had stopped glowing, and his expression was grave. "That was the night that our world was consumed with fire, when water turned into fuel for the fire that he had imagined. It was a terrible thing.

"He decided that his gift was something bad that no one should have. He knew that his gift was genetic, and did not want anyone to have the gift ever again. He killed his entire family--his wife, his two daughters--and then he killed himself."

Father straightened, shifted his shoulders, and sighed. "But one of his children he did not kill. One was very young, about your age, Samuel. And that one was me. This scar"--he pointed to his forehead--"was from when he tried to kill me. It has stretched as I have aged, so it does not look the same as it did. My injury has prevented me from becoming a Maker, since it damaged a part of my brain from when I was very young. But I knew that the gift was within my genetics, and so when I found a woman who also presented the progressing traits of mankind's continually evolving brain, I married her to guarantee that Aldous' gift would spread to a future generation."

He reached over to Mother and gave her hand a squeeze, smiling softly. She smiled back.

He turned back to the boys and said, "Aldous, your grandfather, believed that at the heart of all men was something very dark. He believed that no good would come to men under their own power, and that his gift was a curse to himself and to all on the earth. Others believed and still believe the same. This is why we live in this ship thousands of miles away from anyone. We are hunted because of our gifts. People believe that our gifts make us dangerous.

"But I believe differently. I believe that there is good in man. I believe that at the heart's center is a fire of unceasing light. I believe that, with time and proper training, you, Quinn, are destined to restore humanity, and help it achieve its proper greatness."

Shimmering tears quivered on the brims of his eyes as he placed his hand on Quinn's shoulder. Quinn had the look of an ancient knight, face innocent and bold before a heroic summoning.

Samuel was jealous. He deserved the Gift, not Quinn. Then, a wave of fear coursed through him like an electrical charge. Would Quinn use the gift to hurt him? He thought of all of the terrible stories that Quinn told him at night. There was no limit to what he might do--or what he might have already done. And he became terribly afraid of going to bed that night, more afraid than he had ever been before.

***

That night, Quinn did not tell him any stories after Mother had left the room. Instead, he lay silent for a long time. Several minutes passed. The time became so long that Samuel could not tell if Quinn was awake or if he had fallen asleep without saying anything at all. Samuel was about to turn onto his side, when Quinn spoke at last.

"It's an amazing feeling, you know." Samuel stared up into the dark. "What is?"

"To find out that you are the most important person alive. That you're special."

I'm special too, thought Samuel.

"I mean, once I'm ready, Father says, we will return to Earth and we'll start to fix things. Things will be fixed because of me, because of what I can do."

Samuel didn't respond.

"Don't worry, Samuel," said Quinn. "I'll make sure to save a special place for you when I'm the King of Earth."

This was the first night that Quinn had said something nice to him before they fell asleep. But it still made Samuel uneasy.

"Okay," said Samuel.

There was another stretch of silence, and Quinn finally said, "I can't sleep. I'm too excited. I can't wait to start my training. Father says that there is something very special deep inside of me--and I only need to learn how to fully connect to it."

Samuel was glad that Quinn was happy because it meant that Quinn might not be likely to have nightmares.

In darkness, Samuel said, "I hope you learn it fast."

"I'll be quiet now though," Quinn said. "I know you need to sleep too, so you can do better at your math."

Samuel felt like he was about to cry, but he didn't want to cry. So he squeezed his eyes shut and let his face get hot from anger, and then he rolled over in his bed.

It was a long time before sleep came. He could hear Quinn breathing above him, clearly awake from the inconsistent rhythm.

His restless mind was flooded with thoughts of Quinn. Quinn had always been the favorite. Samuel had always been the little brother. Quinn was still the favorite, this time because he clearly had a special gift.

But Samuel knew that he was special too. He didn't know why yet, but he knew that he was. Father had said so. Maybe when he was as old as Quinn, he would find out what his special talent was.

***

Samuel awakened to a loud, repetitive thudding noise. He had been in very deep sleep and, for a while, he was not convinced that he was awake. In half-sleep, he thought that it was possible that Quinn was making the noise, rocking in his bunk, or making it by striking some object against the wall, another one of his pranks. In half-dream, he desperately felt that he must stay in his cot, under his sheets, at all cost.

But after the third or fourth thud, Samuel emerged into full consciousness, aware at last that it was not Quinn who was making the noise. It was something very large. Something outside of the ship.

He bolted upright in his bunk just as the lights came on in the small cabin space. He saw that Quinn was already up, near the door.

"What is it?" Samuel said.

"I don't know."

Quinn opened the door and went toward their parents' room. Suddenly, the ship rocked to the side, knocking Quinn off of his feet and sending him tumbling across the floor.

Samuel sprang from his bed and rushed to the door. The gravity units must have been knocked out of place, because Samuel felt as though he were walking a steep incline.

Mother and Father burst from their room and gathered up the children.

They made their way to the kitchen and eating area, central to the ship, the safest from any outside harm.

Father said, "Everyone stay here. I'm going up to have a look." He left them at the table, motioning for them to stay still, Mother's

surprisingly powerful arms holding them back.

Father turned and went to the ladder that went up into the cockpit. He placed his hand on one of the rungs, and his foot on another.

Samuel was afraid. He wished for some sort of shelter, for safety, so that he would not become like the dead bodies he had seen. He trembled in fear.

Then with a terrible screeching sound of rending metal and hundreds of gallons of air being sucked into vacuum, the hull tore and the room split in two at the floor, at the ceiling, and at the walls between them and their father. Electrical lines in the structure sparked as they ripped apart and small pieces of debris caught in the whirlwind spiraled about the room threatening to scratch their faces. The wind grabbed at their bodies, tearing them out of their chairs, and away from each other.

And then in sudden airless silence, they were in space. Father was already far away. Samuel could make out his form
in a white suit, one white hand hanging on to a rung of the ladder attached to a jagged white fragment of the ship. All around was the blackness of space, the distant stars like miniscule flecks of dust on black velvet.

Quinn and Mother were closer to him, but the violence of the rupture had sent them floating away from each other, away from him.

Mother looked like a doll submerged in a bath, arms and legs straight, her head a flowing shiny mass of black hair.

Quinn's face was clearly visible to Samuel. His eyes were locked open in fear, but the pupils were obscure. They had already begun to freeze over. The areas around his nose and mouth and eyes were turning blue. His hands clutched weakly at nothing.

Behind the scattered wreckage of the ship, the worm hovered like a cloud. It sat motionless amongst the stars; at first it didn't even seem alive. Its body caught the dim starlight but did not reflect the light in the way that a normal object would. It seemed to be visible by a greenish absorption of light into its flesh, as dark as the expanse of space itself. Its eternal tail was wound in a knot so large that Samuel could not find its edges.

Samuel was warm. He did not feel the vacuum of space pulling at his saliva. He did not feel the cold creeping into his mouth or his eyes or his nose. He was safe.

He reached out his hand to touch a smooth, glassy surface, invisible before him.

The pieces of the ship slowly spiraled away. The slow beast lumbered through space and devoured the bodies as it found them. Red crystals of shattered blood sparkled in deep contrast to its dark flesh.

Samuel did not want this gift.

He squeezed his eyes shut.

He imagined his family alive. He imagined his father talking, laughing. He imagined his mother, holding him to her chest, brushing his hair. He even imagined Quinn, shaking his sandy brown hair out of his face.

Samuel opened his eyes, but there was nothing--nothing but the worm, and the silent wreckage, and the frozen shards of bodies.

Why is it not working?

He remembered his father's words: you must search deep inside yourself.

Samuel searched deep. He probed the deepest part of his heart that he could find.

And then, only distinguishable by its blacking out of the stars, a dark hand reached toward Samuel--a sinister hand with a thousand fingers, colder and darker than the deepest night.

The End.

Case #95194
Jonathan Anderson

J.D. Anderson resides in Washington State with his wife and daughter, working as a teacher. He contributes music reviews to the extreme-metal website Teeth of the Divine.

Hope from the Eternal Damned

Patrick Jagielski

Physician: Dr. Lichten
6428-SED41

CHEVEYO WAS RUNNING AS FAST AS HE COULD, he couldn't let the elk get away. He sped past the trees, jumped over ferns, and bounded over streams. The elk was fast and on the verge of escaping; Cheveyo had to finish this soon or it would flee for good. Cheveyo glanced to his left and found his solution – a ledge that led uphill and dropped at a sudden cliff. The elk was running past the bottom of that cliff, and Cheveyo would have a clear shot from above.

Without delay, Cheveyo darted left and ran up to the top of the ledge. He took out his bow to prepare for his shot, but saw another man out of the corner of his eye. It was too late for the other man though – their tribe's code for hunters give Cheveyo the kill. Cheveyo was closer, had a clear shot, and obstructed the other man's line of fire. He ignored the other man and drew his bow. The elk was running below – the time was now. He crouched down, took aim, and released his bow. The arrow soared towards the elk, properly led. Cheveyo's eyes rose, waiting for the kill....

The arrow struck prematurely at the base of a tree. Cheveyo watched the elk dash away, dispirited with yet another failed attempt. "You didn't lead it properly," the man from behind him said.

Cheveyo looked over and recognized Wemotin, a fellow hunter in his tribe. "I led it perfectly, only the tree got in the way."

"Part of properly leading your shot is making sure the arrow hits its target," Wemotin laughed. His voice was soothing, compassionate. "Next time, be sure to take an extra moment to plan your shot. The river isn't far from here. You could have had a clear shot near the river if you had waited. Come, let's retrieve your arrow and see if the arrowhead is still intact."

"I don't need your help," Cheveyo said as he started his way down the ledge to the arrow. "You're always quick to give criticism. Why don't you just worry about yourself? Shouldn't you be concerned about bringing in more carcasses for the Potlatch? The new moon is coming soon."

The Potlatch was held every twelve new moons to celebrate the coming of the harvest by bringing in as much hunted carcasses as possible, and was truly the prime event of the Nomish tribe. The best musicians would play their drums and rattles while singers chant their songs in rhythmic trances. Dancers would dance to their most celebrated god – the Spirit of the Seahawk, called Wahkan – but only the most talented dancer symbolized Wahkan. Viewing such a performance is considered a high honor. All tribes near and far were invited to bring their best performers and participate in the celebration.

The most important part of the Potlatch was the Dustu-Makya. Just as the best crops are harvested for the Potlatch, the best hunter is selected to be trained for leadership. The best hunter is determined by whoever gathers the most carcasses, illustrating their skill in hunting. This hunter then becomes a full member of a small but elite group of hunters in the tribe called the Makya.

The leader of the Makya is called the Makya-Cha. When the Makya-Cha steps down from his position or dies, the best hunter is elected from the Makya to become Makya-Cha. Cheveyo thought of his father, who was a hunter in the Makya before he died. If only he had his father's skills in hunting, he could be chosen to become part of the Makya. But he was considered one of the worst hunters in his tribe, hopeless to even dream of such a high honor.

"How much have you gathered so far?" Cheveyo asked.

"I've hunted enough for now. I'm looking to see if any struggling hunters need help, and it looks like you do. Let's kill that elk together, we're stronger as two than alone."

"No, I don't need your help," Cheveyo said. "I want this kill to count for myself." He bent down to retrieve his arrow and saw that the arrowhead was broken. He threw it in disgust.

"I see you didn't take the time to fix your tomahawk," Wemotin said, pointing at Cheveyo. "The binding isn't tight enough, and the stone isn't honed to the right size. You'll never kill anything with that."

"It wasn't worth the time. You know how long it takes." Cheveyo glanced down at his waist where his tomahawk hung on his leather pelted jerkin. "It does all I need it to do."

"If I may return your original question, how many carcasses have you gotten for the Dustu-Makya so far?" Wemotin asked. Cheveyo hesitated, ashamed of his total. "I have some foxes…. and a wolf," he added at the end. It was a lie, he didn't have a single carcass.

"The wolf is good, but the foxes won't count much toward the total. If you truly want to be chosen, you'll have to gather a lot more than that. Let me help you."

"Why are you so eager to help? Don't you want to be chosen? "I do," Wemotin confessed. "I want to join the Makya as much as the next hunter. But I understand the importance of gathering as much meat as possible for the other tribes. Many of the smaller tribes aren't as fortunate as us, and depend on our surplus meat for their supply. If I help our fellow hunters, we can gather more than just me alone."

"But we've never been short on meat for the other tribes. So I'd rather do my hunting on my own and get the credit for myself," Cheveyo stubbornly continued.

"Suit yourself, Cheveyo." Wemotin started to walk back and turned around to face Cheveyo. "You lack patience, my friend. Patience and compassion."

"You don't know what you speak of, Wemotin," Cheveyo said as he walked toward the river. Perhaps he could find a better tomahawk stone, or even that elk. But more importantly, he hoped to find the herbs he needed for his sister's medicine. "You cannot help me," he whispered to himself.

***

Cheveyo thought of his older sister, Pivari, as he went towards the river. He'd be able to find the bitterroot he needed to complete Pivari's medicine. "He knows nothing about Pivari and her fever," Cheveyo spoke to himself as he spotted the bitterroot by the flowing water. "She's been sick with fever for almost eight moons. She should have either died by now or gotten better. No one can survive that long with a fever." Cheveyo knew the medicine wasn't healing her, but he couldn't bring himself to say it. It was all that was keeping her alive, and it was all he could do for her. "I know my tomahawk is the worst in the tribe, I know I'm the worst hunter, but he doesn't know I have to take care of Pivari. Family comes first."

Cheveyo recently realized he'd been good at spotting the herbs he needs for medicine – much better than his skill in hunting. If he could, he'd stop being a hunter and gather herbs to practice medicine with the tribe. But his sister wouldn't allow it, the only family he had. Pivari, fourteen years older than Cheveyo, raised him up. Their mother died giving birth to Cheveyo, a fact Pivari

never seemed to forget or forgive. She had grown from a spiteful youth into an angry woman, and Cheveyo preferred gathering herbs alone than tending to her needs at home. She regularly accosted him for the poor hunter he was, "You're bringing shame to our family name," she'd say. "Why aren't you being selected in the Dustu-Makya like our family used to?" But Cheveyo couldn't neglect her need for medical attention, and he was the only one that could give it. "I can't stop taking care of her," he assured himself. "Saving my sister is more important than the Dustu-Makya."

Cheveyo finished gathering the bitterroot and placed it in his satchel. As he rose from the ground, he saw an elk straight ahead of him drinking water from the river. Is this the same elk from before, he thought? As he drew his bow, he saw it wasn't. There was a strange glow to this elk, with dark blue vein-like webs running up its antlers, and a mist shrouding beneath it.

Suddenly, the elk's face snapped up, roared a high-pitched screech, and ran back to the forest. I can't let this one get away, Cheveyo thought as he jumped into the river, swam across to the other side, and chased after it. The elk had graceful form, and left a strange blue aura behind him as it ran. His antlers seem to glow the more it ran. Just as Cheveyo thought the elk was as good as gone, it dashed into a nearby cavern. Yes, he's trapped now. Cheveyo reached the cavern out of breath, but hopeful. As he walked further in, the cavern came to an abrupt halt, with nothing in sight. "But where did it go!?" he yelled, frustrated over his lost kill.

"I don't think you'll be too upset that you lost this one elk once you leave this cave, hunter."

"Who is that?" Cheveyo asked, pulling out his tomahawk.

The booming voice from nowhere laughed when Cheveyo pulled out his tomahawk. "You can put that piece of work back from where you got it. A primitive tool like that won't help you here."

Cheveyo hesitated, wary to trust this unseen stranger. He lowered his tomahawk, but still held it tightly. "Who are you? Show yourself! I can't see you." His voice trembled, afraid of the unknown.

"I am your answer. I can help you with-"

"Stop, you can't help me! I don't know who you are. I've had enough of people not understanding me."

"I know of your sister, Cheveyo, unlike that selfish Wemotin. Anyone can see he's still trying to help himself. I know about Pivari's fever, and I know of your pressure to join the elite hunters called the Makya when the new moon arrives."

"How do you know all that?"

"Let us just say I possess qualities that are not of your kind. In fact, I am not really your kind."

"Like Wahkan, the Seahawk god?"

The booming voice let out a long laugh, leaving Cheveyo unsettled. "Your pitiful god who feigns benevolence? No. I am not like Wahkan, whose incessant tests of worthiness cause more tribulation than altruism. I am a god, who can help you now and ask nothing in return."

"How do I know you can actually help me?" Cheveyo asked. Despite his fear of this god, he was starting to feel hopeful, his first sign of hope in years. He never told anyone about Pivari. No one cared. If he did actually know all this, perhaps he does have the power to help.

"I can get rid of Pivari's fever. I know how that has been consuming your life. You'll then have the time to hunt the most carcasses for the Dustu-Makya."

"Even if Pivari is cured and I can spend my days hunting, how will I have the most carcasses by the new moon? I'm not a good hunter. I haven't a single carcass, my bow skills are novice at best, and my tomahawk will fall apart any day." He paused and softly added, "I don't even know if I want to be a hunter! My sister just wants me to."

"You do want to be a hunter. It's in your blood, and so is triumph." The end of the cavern started to shine the same dark blue that elk's antlers shown. "Which hand do you favor most?"

Cheveyo nearly fell in amazement. How did the blue light emit from the rock? He tried to catch his voice, but was too startled. He merely raised his left hand and managed to stutter, "Th – this one…"

An even brighter light began to form an image of a left hand in the center of the rock at the end of the cavern. Below the hand, another brighter light began forming an outline of a tomahawk stone. Cheveyo had never seen a better shape for a tomahawk stone than this. If he could get this stone as it was outlined, it would be perfect. He'd hardly have to do anything himself except bind it on his handle with twine.

"I will remove your sister's fever," the voice boomed. "And I can give you the perfect tomahawk stone, here." The light outlining the tomahawk stone burned a bright white, blinding Cheveyo, and suddenly dimmed. A stone lightly fell at his feet, close enough for Cheveyo to confirm the perfect tomahawk stone. Still, it did not completely satisfy him.

"But what about my hunting skill?" Cheveyo asked suspiciously. "I may have the time and the best weapon, but I still need to gain the most carcasses. How will you help me there?"

"I can give you the skill if you place your hand on cavern wall. Do this and I guarantee you will be chosen at the Dustu-Makya."

This is it, this is what I need, Cheveyo though. The tribe elder once warned the whole tribe to be wary of such easy promises from spirits. "But the elder doesn't know my problems, just like Wemotin doesn't," he yelled defiantly. "Yes!" he roared in relief, agreeing to the unknown spirit. He picked up the tomahawk stone, light as a feather but as durable as metal, and dropped it in his satchel. He dashed to the glowing blue wall and threw his left hand at the imprint.

Immediately, the light on the wall focused only on the hand imprint and shone brightly at Cheveyo, blinded again. Dark blue veins appeared on his fingertips and began crawling up to his forearm. Cheveyo could feel aggression, hate, and violence begin to overtake him. He tried to suppress those feeling, but soon gave in. The unknown spirit began to laugh, and Cheveyo realized he had been tricked. He tried franticly to remove his hand, but it was stuck to the wall as the light began to seep into him. The spirit took firm control of his mind, but not entirely. It wiped Cheveyo's impulse to eradicate the spirit, the most important thing to suppress. But it was not enough for the spirit to control Cheveyo's intentions.

Not yet at least.

***

Cheveyo walked out of the cavern and shielded his eyes from the sun as they adjusted to the daylight. As soon as he could see, he noticed his hand pulsing with dark blue veins that started in his fingertips and ran all the way up to his forearm. I'll need to cover this up when I get back to the tribe, he thought. If these scars are the only price I have to pay, I'll be forever thankful.

As he was making his way back to his sister, Cheveyo suddenly heard a branch snap. He glanced to his left, and made eye contact with a startled elk with its foot on a broken branch. Cheveyo wondered if this was the elk that got away, but it didn't matter, he desperately needed a successful hunt. His mind focused on killing the elk, unknowingly allowing the spirit within to act on this intention to kill.

In an instant, his mind slipped as if someone was working through him. He knew he wouldn't have enough time to draw his bow and kill the elk – it would run out of reach before he even notched the arrow. Instead, his hand, out of his control, reached to his tomahawk with its new stone. As he subconsciously raised the tomahawk above his head, he could feel how flawlessly the weight was distributed. He flexed his arm and threw it, releasing his hand at the precise moment. Cheveyo watched as the tomahawk made two rotations in the air and landed the sharpened stone directly between the elk's eyes.

"Ha!" Cheveyo yelled, running towards the fallen elk. "Perfect hit!" As he struggled to rip out his tomahawk deep within the elk's head, he was stunned at the sheer perfection of his tomahawk throw. There was no wobble or falter on its lethal flight toward the elk, only straight and true. He had never seen a tomahawk drive so deeply into a target before, not even by the Makya-Cha. Never in his life did he dream of being such a lethal force. He glanced at his flexed hand trying vainly to remove the tomahawk and concluded the spirit indeed told the truth. When he let his mind slip, he let the spirit take over his actions.

Excited with his newfound ability, he grabbed the elk and brought it over his shoulder, the brute strength coming from the spirit. "Pivari will be pleased with this kill. I'll skin and salt the elk after I give her the medicine – and perhaps the spirit will have cured her fever."

Cheveyo approached his tribe's village minutes later, still carrying the elk. Many of his fellow tribesman and hunters glared, pointed, and whispered of the clean cut on the elk's head and Cheveyo's sudden strength to carry an entire elk himself. Cheveyo noticed their whispers, and was glad for it. Let them spread the word of my strength, it will help me even more in being chosen in the Dustu-Makya.

At last he saw the longhouse and entered through the leather tarp door. Their tribe, and their neighboring tribes, lived in longhouses instead of the teepees of the Eastern tribes. The cedar trees in their region were long, sturdy, and plentiful – perfect for cedar planks used to build their shelter. Cheveyo lived in the community longhouse, which housed most of the tribe's population. Only the most esteemed families in the tribe were granted their own longhouse, and had to be appointed by the Chief himself. Cheveyo walked down the center aisle, nearly one hundred feet long, and arrived at his and Pivari's meager segment of the longhouse.

Their section was surrounded by leather tarps his father had hunted for years ago. In the center was the fire pit, issuing more smoke than heat, directly under a hole in the ceiling to allow the smoke to escape. In the corner were two straw mattresses. Pivari lay on one of them facing away from him. "Is that you?" Pivari demanded upon hearing Cheveyo enter. She turned over to look at him.

"Yes, it's me, sister" he said as he proudly dropped down the dead elk. "Look what I hunted today. Are you proud? I've finally-"

"Give me my medicine first," she interrupted as she sat up. The sparse light from the fire dimly lit her face so that Cheveyo could see. She had once been very pretty. You look just like your mother, the other tribesmen would say. But as the years wore on, Pivari had grown bitter. Her dimples and high cheekbones turned to a sullen dough face with botches and boils. Because she hardly left the longhouse, she had grown larger, her clothes now too tight to wear. She had also once been a marvel of a storyteller, captivating the longhouse neighbors around their fire. But she had lost that charm for stories as well. Her tales of glory, life-long lessons, and spirits turned to bitter japes and insults directed at Cheveyo.

"Yes, sister. You must be in pain." He removed his satchel, dropped to his knees, and began grinding the bitterroot in his wooden mortar and pestle. As he was making her medicine, his mind drifted to the Dustu-Makya. As much as Cheveyo loved his sister, he started feeling the urgency to hunt so he could be chosen to join the Makya. He wouldn't be able to both skin the dead animals and hunt enough in time for the next full moon. He hoped the bitterroot he was grinding would be the last, fulfilling the promise of the spirit within him just as it already enhanced his hunting. When he finished grinding the bitterroot, he poured the powder into a clay cup of water, hoping for her fever to end. "Here, drink this."

She took the cup and drank greedily, giving a shudder once it was all down. "Too bitter, your medicine doesn't work – I still have my fevers."

"If you didn't take it, you wouldn't be alive," he said instantly. Pivari stared at Cheveyo, who never talked back to his sister. "Trust me this time, I think it'll work. I'm trying something new, just give it some time."

After a pause of ignoring her brother, Pivari looked down at the dead elk by the dying fire. "When are you going to skin and salt your elk?"

"I was hoping that you could, sister. I have much more to hunt if I want to be chosen at the Dustu-Makya. The new moon will be upon us soon, and I have little time to catch up to the other hunters seeking to be chosen. Especially if I'm to continue getting your medicine to hold your fever back."

"Nonsense. My place isn't to take care of your kills. A true hunter will clean his own carcasses, not his dying sister!" she said. "And I thought this medicine was supposed to cure me this time," she added vindictively.

Cheveyo knew he would be put down by his sister, but he could never prepare himself to feel the guilt each time she accused him of wrongdoing or shortcomings. "But all the other hunters eligible for the Dustu-Makya have their family helping them after their hunts. Please, sister, I won't be able to be chosen without your help." He looked at her pleadingly, wanting her to finally be proud of what he accomplished and work together in his achievement.

"No. They aren't real hunters like our family. Your father didn't have his women clean his carcasses, and he was a true and skilled hunter. The man in our family has one duty only – to provide. You'll never be good enough to provide."

He rose and pointed his finger at Pivari. "But I am providing," he insisted.

Pivari finally got up from her straw mattress and slapped Cheveyo's face. "I am the oldest in our family. What evil spirit has possessed you to speak to me that way?"

Cheveyo's mind began to be drawn back, the hunter's spirit taking form. He grew more aware of their small section of the longhouse, like a mist rising and revealing what was truly there for the first time. Half-woven baskets were on the dirty rugs that hadn't been tightened in months, the dying fire hadn't been properly tended since Cheveyo had done it yesterday, almost no water in the clay water jugs, leather jerkins and cloth that was meant to be washed in the river many moons ago. "Is this the first time you got up today?" Cheveyo heard himself say.

"You dare, brother? I am sick with fever. You come in here and expect your dying sister to tend to all these tasks and do your own skinning?" Pivari squinted her eyes and muttered, "You're a shame to our family. Bring me what water we have left; I have a thirst."

"You've been dying for more moons than I can count on my hands. You spend more time shaming me than helping me." Cheveyo looked around further and noticed that not a single thing had changed since he left that morning. "I'm right, aren't I? You've been laying down all day, just like you have all these moons." You don't need her anymore, the new voice inside him said.

"Are you calling me weak? I've survived all these moons. I'm the one who brought you up after you killed our mother. I've made you who you are."

"You've made me into nothing, just like the nothing you are." Without her, you can hunt all you will need to be chosen this year at the Dustu-Makya.

"If you want to go and hunt more, go do it. All you are is a killer, Cheveyo. You were a killer when you first entered this world, and you're a killer now."

Cheveyo was stricken, his heart wounded. Those words struck him because they couldn't be truer. He was a killer at birth, and despite his struggles as a hunter in the past, he knew that's all he was now. Kill her, the hunter within whispered. She's right, embrace who you are. You can be the best killer in this tribe. But only if she is gone. Any resistance to the spirit within him snapped, unable to control the hunter within. He accepted who he was, and let the killer take over.

"Are you going to cry, little brother? Like you used to every night? Praying to the spirits to bring your mother back? That doesn't solve your problems, brother. It never did!" Pivari said as Cheveyo silently reached for a leather blanket. "What are you doing? What's wrong with your arm? Why is it pulsing blue?"

Cheveyo grabbed the blanket, rapidly wrapped it around Pivari's face, and pulled tight – not a sound was made. "You're right, sister," Cheveyo whispered behind her ear as he kept pulling the blanket tight, suffocating her. "I am a killer, just like you raised me to be."

Pivari's response was muffled and unintelligible, nobody could hear her struggle. She tried to reach up to remove the blanket, but Cheveyo wrapped his legs around her arms, inhibiting any movement or retaliation.

"I've found somebody who could do something about it, and he promised I'll be chosen at the Dustu-Makya at the new moon," he continued to whisper. "No one will think twice of your death. With no evidence of a struggle and nobody to hear me kill you, they'll all think you finally died of your fever, like you should have moons ago."

As Cheveyo continued to pull on the blanket behind her, Pivari started jerking. On the brink of his sister's death, Cheveyo's conscious barely reemerged and questioned the spirit in a whisper, "Pivari is family, surely there's another way." Not if you want to hunt enough for the Dustu-Makya, the spirit responded. She's held you back for years. She's as good as dead with her fever. Let me kill her, and I promise you'll be chosen. Thinking of the Dustu-Makya, he succumbed to the spirit once again.

When Pivari jerked her last, Cheveyo checked her pulse and felt nothing. He laid the dead body on the mattress, Wait until morning to announce her death, say she died in the middle of the night.

Cheveyo finished the day skinning his dead elk and preserving the meat with salt. He felt no regret toward his actions, the spirit starting to grasp a tighter hold of him. He went to sleep at peace knowing he'd have enough time to hunt all he needed for the Dustu-Makya.

***

The day of the new moon had come. Every person in the tribe had his or her task – preparing the bonfire, setting the stage for the dancers and storytellers, cooking the vast quantity of food to feed thousands. The neighboring tribes had traveled from miles away for the festival, setting up their temporary camps nearby.

Cheveyo was just returning from one last hunt when he came across Sootan, his tribe's Shaman leader. "So, there's word that you're favored to be chosen at the Dustu-Makya this year, Cheveyo. Are these whispers true? Do you think you have hunted the most? They say you hunt like a possessed man," he laughed as he put his arm around Cheveyo's shoulder.

Cheveyo's improved hunting skills were no secret. At all hours of the day, the tribe would see Cheveyo hauling in dead bear, elk, deer, even a baby whale all by himself! "I certainly hope so, I have not heard of anyone hunting more than I have."

"You must be saddened about your sister passing, unable to see your recent achievement."

It hadn't even crossed Cheveyo's mind, he had almost forgotten about Pivari's burial unless Sootan had reminded him. Nearly all the tribe had forgotten too, with the upcoming Potlatch. "Yes, I am deeply saddened," he responded, feigning a rehearsed sigh of mourning. I pray to our spirits every night asking her to see me tonight."

"She will be, Cheveyo. The dead do not cease living. Rather, their spirits become one with our surroundings. And those spirits surely have blessed you as of late – I hear that you hunted an infant whale all by yourself. I've never heard of a single man to do that himself." "Call it a stroke of luck that I happened to chance upon." They reached their tribe's camp, "I must go, Sootan. I have much to prepare for tonight. May the spirits bless you."

"And you, Cheveyo."

As the sun reached its precipice and began to lower as the day went on, the Potlatch festival began. Children ran around playing games, chasing each other. Girls played with their homemade dolls while trading homemade clothes to fit their dolls. Boys fought with wooden sticks, trying to impress the girls nearby

to no avail. The adults went to all corners of the camp going to different vendors eating new foods and trading baskets, painted pottery, art, precious stones, animal hides, and whale oil to light lanterns. The food vendors gave out roasted elk, fish, breads, corn, and even bear, all using spices unique to each tribe. Everyone in attendance commented on each tribe's unique signature spice while the merchants made trade arrangements for them. In the streets, performers beat their drums, played their horned flutes, sang their chants, danced in rhythm of the music, and storytellers told their tales of marvel and virtue. Each of the tribes' elders met under covered tarps, smoking tobacco and herbs from all over, sharing stories and wisdoms only the most experienced in life can share.

The Potlatch festival of the new moon was a festival of prosperity and sharing with their fellow man. Not only does it symbolize prosperity, it was also a revered time of peace. Wars hadn't been fought among these tribes for generations, and none have been as prosperous as they are now.

Cheveyo sat next to the central ceremonial fire, now an orderly pile of firewood waiting to be lit when the sun sets and the new moon rises. The fire was the centerpiece of the Potlatch festival – the music and dancing which paid homage to their god: the Seahawk spirit, called Wahkan. The most important event took place at the central ceremonial fire, and since the Dustu-Makya is the most anticipated, it is the last event of the festival. "Pathetic, all of them," Cheveyo spoke to himself of the visiting tribes. "They come here, taking our goods, and what do we get in return? Nothing. We'd be stronger if we just kept to ourselves." The blue veins on his forearm pulsed more than ever. He wasn't sure if this was his own thought or the thought of the spirit within him.

Cheveyo remained sitting near the ceremonial fire, waiting patiently as the sun began to set. He knew he would be chosen during the Dustu-Makya and join the coveted Makya huntsmen, there was no way he could lose. He had brought in more carcasses than any other champion before. He trusted the hunter spirit inside him, and let him take over more often than not lately. As Cheveyo pondered this, the low drums started beating and the shrill blaring of the horns blew, signifying the beginning of the main events. When everyone had gathered around the unlit fire, the horns and drums ceased. All conversations ceased immediately as the Chief of Cheveyo's tribe rose up to spoke, standing next to the fire. It was tradition that the Nomish Chief would begin the ceremony, welcoming each tribe and telling the story of the Nomish origins for those who were new to the Potlatch. The full moon's light shined down on the Chief, showing his elaborate headdress of feathers and face paint. He was holding a lit torch.

"As Chief of the Nomish tribe, I thank you all for attending our Potlatch. For more moons than I have lived through, our tribes have been at peace. This peace has enabled our tribes to work together and make each other stronger, wiser, and well fed. Our festival this year is no different. I am proud to lead the Nomish tribe, and I am proud to live among you all." The Chief glanced to his left, and the audience glanced in turn. "That totem over there by the sea, that totem is of our tribe's god: The Seahawk whom we call Wahkan. The totem represents the story of our tribe's origin. When our tribe first settled in the very land we are sitting now, they were struck with the curse of famine. No matter what could be done, our most skilled hunters or gatherers could not bring home meat or herbs for sustenance. Just as the tribe was going to starve, a flock of sea hawks flew out to meet our famished ancestors. The largest of the hawks landed next to our Chief and asked 'Why do you all starve this way and not search for food?' And our Chief responded, 'Our tribe has been cursed with famine. We struck a deal with an evil spirit; he was too tempting. Our old land was destroyed in war and the spirit told us of the land out west by the sea. The sea hawk then went on to say, 'Evil spirits will offer the needy and distressed a solution to their problems, but at a great cost. They feed off of chaos and despair. I do not have such wicked, selfish intentions- I'm not a malevolent spirit, but rather can offer you abundant food as long as you give me something in return. I will give you an abundance of food as long as you never hunt a single sea hawk and always give your excess food to the neighboring tribes just as I gave you food in your time of need.'

"The old Chief knew he was unwise to accept the evil spirit's offer, and learned true prosperity would come when doing the long, hard way with this benevolent sea hawk spirit. 'Yes, we vow to never hunt a single sea hawk and to give generously to our neighbors.' For four seasons, sea hawks would grab fish from the sea and drop them at our ancestor's feet. During that time, they learned to hunt and farm the land properly. Ever since that day, our tribe vowed to never let our neighbors grow hungry or weak, and it has made us all prosperous."

The Chief looked down and then glanced at Cheveyo. After a short pause, he threw the torch into the firewood, and a blaze instantly fired up, spreading its light around the festival. "Let the Potlatch begin!"

The cheering roared as the Chief walked away from the fire and the dancers moved in. Cheveyo watched as the drums and horns began their incessant rhythmic tunes and the dancers danced

in unison. Each performance told its own story, and each tribe performed at least once. He thought they were all pathetic, all these tribes depend on the Nomish and they mention their tribes' prosperity as their own. If I were Chief, I'd end it.

Pipes from each tribe were passed around, each featuring the tribe's special herb, and ended at the Nomish Chief. When Cheveyo

saw the last pipe end with his Chief, he saw him rise again signaling the night's last event: the Dustu-Makya.

"Thank you for your wonderful performances today, neighbors," the Chief began to say. "Of all the Potlatches I've seen through my many years; each one is more entertaining than the last." After a brief pause and a nod at the Makya-Cha, the leader of the Nomish hunters, the Chief exclaimed, "Now begins the most important event of the evening. The Dustu-Makya!" All roared in approval, slapping the logs they sat on or clanking their rattles. "As you all know, we choose the hunter who has brought in the most meat by the new moon. That man will then be a part of the Makya, our esteemed group of select hunters training for leadership in our tribe. Each of our hunting leaders is selected from this group when the previous leader either dies or steps down. It is the Nomish tribe's greatest honor. And this year couldn't be any more exciting, as we've broken many records."

Cheveyo's spirits soared in satisfaction, his forearm pulsing blue. This is it, his name will be chosen at any second. No lone man could beat his weight of thirty-nine stone worth of meat. It broke the previous record by 6 full stone!

"Without further delay," the Chief continued "we are proud to announce that our selection this year is a man who has overcome much in recent days. When things seemed at the ultimate low for him, he put his head down, trusted in the spirits, and hunted his heart out!"

Cheveyo's heart was beating fast, hardly able to contain the anticipation.

The Chief paused with a smile on his face and exclaimed, "This man brought in a record thirty-nine stone worth of meat, and is none other than our tribesman, Cheveyo!" The audience erupted in cheer, the drums beat, and everyone around Cheveyo pat his back in congratulations. Cheveyo rose, his spirits elated. He had done it, We have done it, the spirit inside his said. Cheveyo walked up to his Chief and linked his left arm with his Chief's, the tribe's way of salutation. The Chief smiled at Cheveyo, proud of his record haul. But when he saw Cheveyo's left forearm, he saw the unmistakable blue pulsing veins. His smile instantly dropped and whispered to Cheveyo as they unwound their left arms, "May you one day return back to the light, child."

Cheveyo was so immediately shocked he couldn't bring himself to respond, or rather was forced not to respond. As more of the audience surrounded Cheveyo when his Chief left, he saw the weary man walk over to the Makya-Cha and whisper in his ear, grabbing his left forearm and making lines with his fingers. They both nodded and the Chief returned to the fire.

The Chief stood next to the fire and blew a screeching whistle, abruptly halting the audience's cheers. The Chief's whistle brought immense dread to Cheveyo, and could feel it lumped in his throat. "I said before," the Chief said and paused, "I said before that we had broken records. We in fact broke more than just the thirty-nine stone. We have another member of our tribe's hunters that brought in forty-two stone." The audience "ooohed" in surprise. Cheveyo was shocked. How was this possible? Who could possibly have brought in more than me, than my hunter spirit inside me?

"This man certainly did not take the easy path," the Chief continued, "but he did take the right path. While he had no intentions to be selected in this year's Dustu-Makya, he had the honest intention for the welfare of our hunters, our tribe, and your tribes. He had the patience to train each of our tribe's hunters, thus making the entire group more productive in the meat they come home with. Not only is he patient and an effective teacher, but he had the compassion to act selflessly. These are the traits of a true leader, and a hero. We should all be inspired by his actions." The audience took well to this introduction, giving a louder applause in anticipation of who it is. But Cheveyo knew who it was, and the anger brewed deep inside him, the veins in his arm pulsing darker.

After a short pause, the Chief roared, "For the first and only time in history, I am more than proud to name Wemotin as the Dustu-Makya's second selection! Through his patience to teach and his compassion for us all, he embodies the true symbol of our tribe, of the great Sea Hawk spirit we owe our prosperous culture to, and of the perfect leader. Effective immediately, he is not only an official member of the Makya, but the sole front-runner to become our next hunting leader, the Makya-Cha!"

The audience roared again, louder than before. They ran to Wemotin and hoisted him up in the air making circles around the fire and chanting his name. Cheveyo, meanwhile, walked away from the fire. Forgotten, alone. He stomped over towards the sea and said to the spirit hunter within, "You lied! I didn't get selected!"

But we did win, somebody else won with you. I did as I told you, the spirit said to Cheveyo.

"It should have been only me! They've already forgotten me; they're only cheering for Wemotin! That's not fair, where's my celebration? I should be the next Makya-Cha! I can hunt better than him." He continued to rage until he came across the Sea Hawk totem.

"Damn all you spirits! You give us false hope and give us nothing!" he roared. He looked up at the great Sea Hawk his tribe worshipped and he felt the hate flow through him, starting from his pulsing forearm. He grabbed his tomahawk, lifted his hand in the air, let his mind release as he'd done hundreds of times in the past week, and threw his tomahawk at the totem. The tomahawk struck perfectly in the totem pole's wood in-between the Sea Hawk's eyes.

Cheveyo collapsed to the ground, leaning on the totem and cried out in frustration. He began to doubt letting the hunter spirit in him. What did it gain him? He was chosen to join the Makya and had proven to have the best hunting ability, but futile now that Wemotin was primed to be Makya-Cha. "And meaningless after I killed Pivari and betrayed my family."

It was not all in vain, the spirit said inside Cheveyo's head. I can still make you leader of the hunters. I can make you Makya-Cha.

"No!" Cheveyo instantly roared back. "I've had enough dealings with your kind. Leave me at once."

It's not quite that simple, friend. You're stuck with me, you let me in. At that moment, Cheveyo's pulsing hand involuntarily grabbed his throat and squeezed so hard he couldn't breathe. Cheveyo was powerless to stop this spirit from choking him. The spirit was starting to be able to control his actions due to Cheveyo submitting so frequently.

"Do you mean to kill me?" Cheveyo was able to squeeze out. No, friend. I don't mean to kill you. I mean to shut you up so you

can listen to me. Just because Wemotin is chosen as the front runner for leadership, doesn't mean he will be the next Makya-Cha.

"What do you mean?"

Much can happen between now and then. With enough people on your side, you can become Makya-Cha instead. Or with enough people dead. A leader cannot lead when he is dead. And killing is exactly what we're good at. Just ask all those animals you killed. Just ask your sister.

Cheveyo hated this spirit for that, but he hated Wemotin more. He hated his fake selflessness, he hated his false sense of omniscience, and he hated how he beat him. "Yes, he couldn't be leader when he is dead."

Let me help you kill him and any who stand in your way. With me, I will make you Makya-Cha. When you're Makya-Cha, you'll end all promises to that false Sea Hawk and cease any charity to the neighboring tribes. With them out of your way, you'll bring more prosperity to your tribe than any before you.

"Yes, yes I want that."

Good, but I will need complete control of your mind and body.

Grant it to me, and you will have those things.

Cheveyo, with nothing left to live for, let go.

The End.

Case #37811

Patrick Jagielski

Patrick Jagielski currently lives in New York City and works in advertising. An avid runner, he races for the New York Harriers and ran in college for Clemson University. If you don't see him running all around New York, he's the guy you see reading and writing on the benches at Riverside Park.

Patrick is currently finishing another short story in the same universe as "Hope from the Eternal Damned" called "Find the Snakes". He is ambitiously taking the two separate stories and combining their future events into his debut novel, starring the protagonist and antagonist of each. You can reach out to Patrick through Twitter at https://twitter.com/SirPatrickJag.

Bestselling Horror US

1   Mr. Mercedes: A Novel - *Stephen King*

2   NOS4A2 - *Joe Hill*

3   The Neighbors - *Ania Ahlborn*

4   Bad Men: A Thriller - *John Connolly*

5   If There Be Thorns (Dollanganger) - *V.C. Andrews*

6   Horns: A Novel - *Joe Hill*

7   A Mate for the Beta - *E A Price*

8   The Source (Witching Savannah, Book 2) - *J.D. Horn*

9   The Alpha's Mate - *E A Price*

10   Doctor Sleep: A Novel - *Stephen King*

Compiled May 1st -May 31st 2014
Amazon.com Kindle Chart

Bestselling Horror UK

1 *Skin Game (Dresden Files) - Jim Butcher*

2 Doctor Sleep: A Novel - *Stephen King*

3 Wolves for the Bears - *E A Price*

4 The Three - *Sarah Lotz*

5 A Book of Horrors - *Stephen King*

6 A Crucible of Souls - *Mitchell Hogan*

7 Dawn of Swords - *David Dalglish*

8 A Mate for the Beta - E A Price

9 Pines - *Blake Crouch*

10 Running from the Vampire into the Arms of the Wolf - *E A Price*

Compiled May 1st -May 31st 2014
Amazon.co.uk Kindle Chart

Group
Therapy
06.14
Welcome to the Hope
Spot & Nancy reviews a
horror collection.

Did I get the memo? Am I aware, you might be thinking to yourself, that I'm writing for a horror magazine? So where did I get my head shoved into a meat grinder, to think that this column should have the word "Hope" in it?

The term comes from a website called TV Tropes as far as I've been able to trace it. It refers to the point in a story (or a life, but don't be surprised if I treat lives as naught but stories we're experiencing firsthand) where the dawn is breaking and the night is flying in retreat. Xe's gotten a second wind or the cavalry is on its way…

And then the night swoops back in on vulture's wings. The second wind runs out. The cavalry are slaughtered like a charge of the Light Brigade. The sands run out, and you are now on the other side of the despair event horizon.

That's the hope spot.

This column is about horror and writing horror. It's going to blend theory with practice, the philosophy of horror with the actual world-and story-building. We might talk about how an existentialist like Viktor Frankl would react to Lovecraft's Mythos, and then start to construct a story that explores Lovecraft through logotherapy, or the concepts of the Look and the Other, or Nietzsche's ubermensch. Those story ideas, by the way, will be free for the taking. Adapt or grab them wholesale as you please. They're yours, they're everyone's.

That's how this boat will usually sail, anyway. Deep Ones might capsize it every now and then and have us do something else. That's the risk of getting sponsored by Cthulhu.

<u>A Partial Theory of Horror</u>

I think that I write horror the best when there's something behind it. When there's some kind of theme, something I'm wrestling with in the story, and I'm not just writing a random story, a sequence of events with conflict and well-rounded characters and things that must not be described.

Now, I'm not saying that this is the One True Way to write horror.

People have a psychological need to experience fear, and whether they satisfy it in an uncontrolled setting or completely ignore it they can still suffer in some form or another. Horror stories are one of a number of modes that allow people to satisfy that need in a controlled setting, so even if you're writing for simple scares and the only thing you're calculating is how much something will terrify your audience, then good on you, dear reader. That approach still takes craft to do well.

What I'm saying is that this is the approach that works best for me, and so this is what I'm going to talk about.

In Practice: My Usual Themes

Probably because I come from a religious background, a lot of my horror stories serve as a metaphor for an experience with the divine. Because this is horror and not inspiration lit, though, what I focus on is the other side of the coin that usually gets forgotten today. "Be not afraid" was a favorite expression of every angel because they were downright terrifying.

"Awful" was originally awe-full: full of awe, worthy of respect or fear. It could be as wondrous as it could be terrifying, and frequently awful things were both.

We could sit here for six articles and talk about what I think about God, but that would be a tangent of unholy length and totally off-topic. Suffice it to say that I think that most of us know somebody, or are a somebody, who experienced something Weird.

There's a rational explanation for most of it. Almost all of it. But then there's that one solitary detail that just can't be figured out, that doesn't make sense under the present paradigm, but to admit that it was anything more than something Weird might also be an exercise in making assumptions.

This is the idea that I play with in many of my horror stories, especially the Lovecraftian ones. The protagonist was hallucinating under the effects of sleep deprivation and the trauma of finding a good friend dead… but then how does his phone have record of making a call after the time of death?

The only other explanation is… It's ridiculous, is what it is. That kind of stuff just doesn't happen. But when you sit down at night and you're all alone and the embers in the fireplace are dying down, you can't quite bring yourself to believe the "rational" explanation

either.

A number of my stories are almost more vignettes or anecdotes than things with plot in them, depending on how strictly you define plot. The stories simply relate experiences, which is one of the reasons why they're usually in the first-person point of view. There are these people who have experienced something, something that they can't make heads or tails of

For obvious reasons, the inexplicable element in my stories is rarely wrapped up. If all stories are Doctor Who then my stories are usually from the point of view of the bystander who's there for only a single episode or even just one scene, and never gets to have the full closure on the incident that the Doctor and his companions always enjoy (for the Whovians out there, the episode Blink would be a good approximation).

So, what lies behind your writing? What gets the clockwork turning and the demons keening in your head?

<u>About R. Donald James Gauvreau</u>

R. Donald James Gauvreau works an assortment of odd jobs, most involving batteries. He maintains a blog at www.whitemarbleblock. blogspot.com, where he regularly posts story ideas, free fiction, and other goodies, including a free guide to comparative mythology that was written specifically with worldbuilding in mind.

He is probably not a spider.

The Best Horror of the Year, Volume Six Editied By Ellen Datlow Night Shade Books, 2014

Twenty-four stories make up this anthology, some from authors I know (meaning that I've read their stuff in the past), and some that are new to me. As usual, it's a mixed bag, but I do have to say it's better than many of Ms. Datlow's previous Best Horror of the Year anthologies, and there were a few entries that actually sent shivers running up my spine. So -- without further ado, I give you

The Best Horror of the Year, Volume Six

First up is "Apports," by Stephen Bacon, proving that old adage that there is indeed no rest for the wicked. In 2006, Mark Fisk's wife divorced him and got custody of their little son.

After the ex-Mrs. Fisk started seeing another man, Fisk tried to do himself in, jumping off of the top of a tower along with his little boy. The boy died, Fisk survived. Not long after Fisk was sentenced to time in a mental institution, the ex-Mrs. Fisk commits suicide. Now a guy known as Cowan is looking for Fisk, for "Old times sake and all that." I have to say that using "Apports" to start the collection was a great idea -- it's an awesome story.

I wasn't nearly as fond of the second story, Dale Bailey's "Mr. Splitfoot," as narrated by Maggie Fox, one of the infamous Fox sisters who became known far and wide for the rapping noises they produced with their joints and for ushering in the age of Modern Spiritualism here in the US. Now on her deathbed, she has a conversation with her dead sister Kate remembering a spirit named Mr. Splitfoot and all of the bad things it made her do. What happens in the story is creepy enough, but for some reason Maggie's persona just didn't do it for me.

Moving on, Nathan Ballingrud's story "The Good Husband" was nice and weird, in which a husband stops another of his wife's suicide attempts when he probably should have let her get on with it. Ewww.

Nina Allan wrote "The Tiger," another very different kind of horror story. A photographer named Croft serves ten years in prison for the sexual assault and murder of a child until a new witness comes forward and clears him. Unfortunately, he can't remember much about that time so he's not sure if he's really innocent or if he actually did it. Now he's out, and meets up with Symes, who goes out of his way to help him, even handing him a new camera. Hmmm.

Up next is a deliciously weird tale that would be a great film if someone could do it right. It's "The House on Cobb Street," by Lynda E. Rucker, and my favorite story in this collection. Vivian and Chris Crane buy a fixer-upper in Athens, Georgia. It isn't long until things start happening in their home, and after a while things start happening to the two of them. But that's not the worst of what's going on in this house, Athens' own urban legend.

If I spill what's in this story, it will totally kill it for anyone who wants to read it, so that's all I'll say except that this is one ferociously creepy and nightmarish tale, kind of surreal and way out there. It's also probably the most well-written story in the book. I loved it.

KJ Kabza's "The Soul in the Bell Jar" seems to be set in an alternate world somewhere. Lindsome Glass, a young girl, comes to stay with her great-uncle Dr. Dandridge at his home while her parents are vacationing around the world. Dandridge is a scientist and a "stitchman," so called because of his work with bodies with reanimated souls, or "vivifieds." She is put under the charge of Dandridge's assistant Chaswick, who clearly specifies where Lindsome may and may not go. Of course, that doesn't stop her from wandering around, stumbling upon things she probably shouldn't see, and getting Chaswick mad at her. Unfortunately for all of them, her curiosity gets the better of her. Aside from the weird science that seems normal in this story, it reads like a tale from the Victorian era; it was just okay.

Much, much better is "Call Out," by Steve Toase, another favorite. A country vet in Yorkshire is called out late at night to tend to a farmer's cow and newborn calf. According to the farmer, the cow had been "cooked" from the inside out after giving birth to her calf, and the "birth waters" had "scorched the floor stone-white clean." Let's just put it this way -- the vet probably should have stayed home. It's another that is wrecked in the telling, so I'll just mention after I read this story, I had to put some time and space between myself and this book, especially since I read this story around 2 a.m. all alone in the house.

Moving back into less horror, more weird territory, next up is Robert Shearman's "That Tiny Flutter of the Heart I Used to Call Love." This one was just plain bizarre, but in a really twisted kind of way, I liked it. Two children grow up in a home where the dad shows little, if any affection for the boy. The brother is ignored while the sister is doted on, getting dolls from her father after he returned from traveling all over the world. Together they participate in a strange ritual of sorts, but first he makes sure she's come to really love her new doll. Freaky.

"Bones of Crow," by Ray Cluley, starts out rather tame then quickly moves into the bizzaro world. Maggie lives in a high block of flats, and whenever she can take a break from her chronically ill father with COPD, she sneaks up to the roof to sneak a smoke. On one such visit, she tosses a lit cigarette and then worries that it might have hit litter, so goes to investigate. She does find litter, but she finds something else on the roof -- four giant eggs. I can't even begin to explain what happens afterwards. It wasn't up there on my top story list, but it was definitely well written.

There's a poem next, "Introduction to the Body in Fairy Tales," by Jeannine Hall Gailey, but I'm not a poetry person so I'll move on to another good one, "The Tin House," by Simon Clark. The owner of this house, so named because it's completely "clad in corrugated tin sheets," went missing six months earlier. Not a clue turned up as to his location, so the case is going into the cold files. A detective is assigned to go to the house and take photos of every room before handing over the keys to the owner's nephew. The author takes his time getting to the meat of this story before we find out what happens next, but it's well worth it.

"The Fox" by Conrad Williams also gave me a nice case of spine tingles, as he tells the story of a family's camping vacation. This is another one I can't divulge much about, but it's bone-chillingly good.

I almost skipped the next story "Stemming the Tide," because of the word "zombies" in the first sentence (I cannot stand zombie stories whatsoever), but I read on. A man takes his significant other to visit the Hopewell Rocks, a place where people can walk on the ocean floor when the tide goes out. The place is filled with people, which the man hates. Before the tide comes back in, the lifeguard shoos everyone out and locks the gates. His girlfriend isn't sure what to expect, but he knows. Very strange, but also pretty good.

Priya Sharma's story "The Anatomist's Mnemonic" about a man who has an obsession with hands, starts out fine, but to be really blunt, I figured out what was going to happen well before I got to the ending. I don't like when this happens. Meh.

I also didn't particularly love Steve Rasnic Tem's contribution, "The Monster Makers," about a "special" family where the kids learn more than they should from their grandfather. And while I have an on-again/off-again relationship with Kim Newman's work, his "The Only Ending We Have," featuring a Janet Leigh stand in for "Psycho" who gets entangled with a real-life mother-son combo, just didn't do it for me. Three not so hots in a row didn't bother me though...the next story picked up the weird thread quite nicely: Derek Künksken's story, "The Dog's Paw" about a new guy in the diplomatic service in Africa learning how things work and how to get along there is beyond eerie. Sadly, not so the case with "Fine in the Fire," by Lee Thomas, where a young boy is left in the dark about his older brother's predilections until he stumbles in on a family secret. It brought back shades of A Clockwork Orange. I wasn't overly keen on Jane Jakeman's "Majorlena," either, about an army Major who shows up out of nowhere in Iraq and leaves the same way.

"The Withering" by Tim Casson is much better fare. Set in 1891, a reporter named Cresswell teams up with a Miss Appleby in Wales to try to save a poor young man named Tobias from the gallows.

He is accused of murdering the woman he loved; it is a relationship Dad wasn't happy about because of the class difference. Let's just say Miss Appleby has a very unique talent for getting to the truth. Aside from the satisfying eeriness of this tale, the author keeps it nicely grounded in time and place. In Neil Gaiman's very short piece, "Down to a Sunless Sea," a mother learns the fate of her son who ran away from home to be a sailor at the age of 12. Short, but truly horrific.

Now entering the final stretch, the last three stories in this book are all pretty darn good. Laird Barron also has a nice story here, "The Jaws of Saturn," which I came across in his The Beautiful Thing That Awaits Us All . Barron is a modern master of weird, and this is one of the stories that showcases why I believe so. With his infamous Broadsword Hotel as the setting for this piece, Barron's story concerns a hitman who doesn't like the aftereffects of the hypnosis his girlfriend is undergoing for quitting smoking and decides to confront the hypnotist. Very bad mistake. As I'm fond of saying, Laird Barron could write copy for cereal boxes and it would be good.

Linda Nagata's entry "Halfway Home" is one I'm glad I didn't read while I was on my long airplane flights over the ocean earlier this month. An American passenger on a overseas flight to LAX meets the passenger next to her from the Philippines, who seems to be faring poorly, but says it's just an allergy to nickel. Their topic of conversation turns to exit strategies and the safety card in the seat pocket, a strange topic of discussion indeed. No one can be prepared for what happens next, though. I have to say that this story turned out to be not at all what I thought it was going to be -- kudos.

And last, but not least, a very Lovecraftian piece comes from Brian Hodge with "The Same Deep Water as You." In a bizarre but very different take on the normal Innsmouth-based story, the Department of Homeland Security hires an "animal whisperer" for a very special purpose at a detainment center where the inmates have been housed since 1928. For people like me who like all things Innsmouth, it's a good one.

I will repeat what I said at the outset ... this installment of Best Horror of the Year is probably the best one so far. I know that horror is in the eye of the beholder, but a majority of the stories in this collection worked well to satisfy my hunger for growing creepiness. In previous installments, that definitely was not the case. This time around Ms. Datlow's anthology is one I can definitely recommend to readers of horror -- most especially those who enjoy more cerebral frights than the kind that are in your face and splattered across pages in an ongoing gore fest. I quite enjoyed this one!

About Nancy:

Nancy is a transplanted native Californian who now lives in Florida with her husband Larry and their two dogs. No, they are definitely not even close to being retirees. Her degrees are in history, she enjoys traveling, pretending she's a chef, Sailor Jerry rum, and more than anything else, since she's a classic introvert, she loves to read.

As a kid, she eschewed all the normal children's books and went straight for the library's mystery shelves, and before she was in her teens she was devouring old pulp and horror novels as well. Many years ago she bought a Penguin edition of Lovecraft's Call of Cthulhu just out of curiosity and her reading habits changed from that moment on, as did the demands on her wallet.

She now reads anything remotely weird, loves translated crime fiction, and serves as a co-moderator at Goodreads' Mystery Crime and Thriller group. Nancy is neither a professional critic nor an English major, but she keeps an online reading journal/blog where she writes about her latest reading adventures.

This review first appeared on Nancy's blog May 30 2014 - more reviews can found on the site at http://www.oddlyweirdfiction. com/

The Unraveling of Victor C. Lewis

Max Sheridan

Loeb was a week out of journalism school when he was approached by a short man in an oil-colored trench coat at Mozel's. The man introduced himself as Cotter and he guessed right away that Loeb, like most of Mozel's early morning clientele, had a diploma and that he wasn't exercising it at the moment. Before Loeb could confirm or deny this, Cotter had paid Loeb's bill and suggested they go back to his office, where Cotter said his inbox was so full he sometimes made paper airplanes out of $10,000 work orders.

Cotter's office was one of fifteen sunless windows in the Melnik Building. Loeb had never heard of the Melnik Building or been in that part of town before. On Cotter's door there was a mail drop at chest level. An engraved brass nameplate said: COTTER PRINT AND LITERARY.

Loeb saw that Cotter didn't have a phone, though Cotter kept a girl out front to do what he didn't know. There were no $10,000 paper airplanes lying about, nothing to indicate what Cotter did for a living. As Cotter's conversation wore on, Loeb began to regret that he'd come at all.

Hours later, in the park, Loeb read through Cotter's proposal again for any suspicious language that might be used later to entrap. But then he remembered they'd only shaken hands—he hadn't signed his name or left any bank details.

Cotter said he'd been asked by an Englishman named Morford to write a piece on a fellow Englishman named Lewis. Both Morford and Lewis were members of the Wildlife Sound Recording Society in London and Lewis had gone missing. Loeb was supposed to fly to England and find Lewis, who had disappeared in the wilds of Norfolk eight months ago. He was to find Lewis and write a feature for the Society documenting his trip. The article would appear in The Whippoorwill, a monthly bulletin put out by the Society's sister organization in Chicago. It was for this reason that Morford had agreed to foot a round-trip ticket on Pan-Am, Cotter had said, and a per diem that would make Loeb's head spin—to give the piece that inimitable American feel.

A PR job, in other words. The only regret Loeb had was that five days out of journalism school he'd already become a copy mule. He went back to the Vanderveer, where he kept a $60 room, and then took Cotter's proposal to Vern's Bar across the street to digest its contents again.

***

The jetlag hit Loeb two days late. It hit him at the Plumbers Arms in Belgravia where he sat over his third pint of bitter discussing Victor C. Lewis with Milton Budge, a fellow birding hack and a friend of Morford.

Unlike Loeb, Budge was happy with his work, so he was jealous of Loeb's beginner's luck in getting assigned such a subject. Of Lewis, however, Budge didn't have much to say, other than that he was the world's greatest bird recordist. Budge also said that Lewis's intense sympathy for fowl had led him to Norfolk, where it was rumored he was trying to snare a Pygmy Nuthatch, a bird so rare in England that its last recorded appearance, during the reign of James I, was contested for centuries thereafter. Lewis, Budge seemed to feel, was convinced that like humans, birds spoke in languages and that the Pygmy Nuthatch was the Rosetta Stone of avian linguistics. Loeb wrote all of this down in shorthand.

"Do you believe that?" Budge asked disgustedly a moment later.

"I don't know," said Loeb.

"Well, have you ever heard a Short-billed Dowitcher cleaning its wings?"

"I don't know anything about birds." "Only Lewis has heard that."

Budge laughed, showing Loeb his big unclean teeth. The next morning Loeb woke at 5:45 in a room he dimly recognized as the luxury suite he'd paid for the afternoon before. In the afternoon light the room had looked dingy and sunken, but now with its morning odors and the curtains down Loeb was afraid of touching his toes to the laminate. He lifted himself out of bed and directly into his slippers and he did his morning push-ups.

An hour or so later, showerless, he ate breakfast in a common room with unemployed English day laborers and recovering addicts of one sort or another. He drank a cup of cloudy brown tea.

He was at Victoria Station by eight o'clock and twenty minutes later he was on a train bound for Great Yarmouth. By midday he was in Pilson Green, in the Broads, a vast estuary on the east coast of England, the last place Lewis had been sighted before his disappearance eight months ago. He put in at the Thume Hotel.

The Thume Hotel was run by a local man named Gough. Gough also charged admission to see his wife, a freak of nature. Loeb paid the extra fee and was invited behind the reception desk and through a heavy curtain. On a pedestal on the other side of the curtain was a glass box. Inside this box sat Mrs. Gough, smoking a long ebony pipe. Legless and armless, Mrs. Gough was simply a torso, and a head. There was an antique oil-burning heater positioned beside her.

Gough invited Loeb for a welcome tea in the Thume's sitting room where Loeb had the sensation of being trapped in an overgrown dollhouse of singular decrepitude. As the two men made their way to a clump of furniture arranged beside a second heater, the short-haired carpet sent up little billows of dust and debris while the floorboards underneath moaned. Whole swathes of Gough's wallpaper had flaked off and now hung low like ripened tropical fruit. One of these touched Loeb on the shoulder and he jumped, thinking he'd just passed through an enormous spider web. He was perplexed to see that Gogh collected the fallen scraps and used them for other purposes, like clogging the many chinks in the walls or balancing the coffee table. They drank their tea hemmed in by a tiny bubble of warmth given off by the heater.

It was here, sitting on Gough's decrepit couch, that Loeb began to see the article taking shape inside his head. Into Lewis's story he would weave a story of cultural differences. After all, who could deny, confronted with such conclusive evidence, that the colonies' victory at Yorktown wasn't also a victory of fundamental domestic values. And how better to comfort the American reader permanently in hock for his central heating, steam cleaner and swimming pool—for that palace of convenience, the modern American kitchen—than to offer him a frank look at the daily squalor his English counterpart lived in? Then Loeb had a chilling thought. Might Lewis have been driven to insanity, as Budge had hinted, by a month of days spent sipping cloudy tea with Gough in Gough's sitting room being tapped on the shoulder by fallen wallpaper?

Later Gough took Loeb upstairs to his room where he demonstrated the hot water and the hot water bottle. He then took Loeb aside to say that in the evenings he moved Mrs. Gough to an ample couch in a comfortable room in the back of the hotel where she received callers in a silk robe. Loeb saw no heater in his room.

***

It was a chilly, dark afternoon and Loeb had ordered a pint of ale at the Thume Pub. He took a seat at a table and was served by a man named Warwick.

At four, when the sun began to set, he realized he'd wasted the afternoon. He couldn't set out in search of Lewis in the dark. He itemized the day's expenses and made a note in his journal that his first day in the field had been a relative success. He'd managed to arrive in Pilson Green by public transport and by a stroke of luck was staying at the same hotel where Lewis had put up just before his disappearance. Warwick had said so. The next day he would set out with Warwick's brother, Cuthbert, who knew the area well. Loeb estimated that with an intelligent approach, and Cuthbert's geographical expertise, they would track Lewis down before the week was out.

The next morning there was a high wind and a low fog, an abominable combination according to Cuthbert and one he wouldn't risk taking the Range Rover out in. So Loeb spent the day in the pub, encouraging locals to reminisce about Lewis. But no one had anything to say. Only one villager, a joiner named Pike, suggested that Lewis might have solved some great mystery, but Pike was known to swallow as much as half a bottle of single malt a night, so Loeb didn't look further into his account.

When the fog rose two days later Cuthbert was waiting for Loeb at the pub at eleven in the morning with his lunch in a bag, the Range Rover purring steadily at the curb. Cuthbert knew where Lewis's bird box was and was willing to take Loeb out to the cabin for the fee they'd agreed on, ten pounds. Any further scouting had to be arranged between them, but it would cost, as it was early winter and the roads likely flooded. Loeb hadn't imagined that a drive out to the cabin and back would be the extent of his investigative reporting. He'd expected Cuthbert to have some ideas of his own. He said, "Do you think he's there then, at the cabin?"
"I think not."

"What do you think then?"

"I think he's dead, long dead," Cuthbert said.

"I doubt this."

"Do you?"

"I doubt Mr. Morford would have paid my flight if he'd exhausted all hope."

Here Cuthbert offered his own expertise, a geographical assessment of the land and its decompositional peculiarities, the poor odds of a body being found there a month after it was too late. Loeb shrugged at this and said, "But I suppose we'd get an idea of what happened at the cabin if nothing else."

"Maybe."

"If it's ok with you, I'd like to check the cabin first." "You owe me ten pounds then."

They reached the cabin at three due to the bad roads. The sun was already threatening to sink and they needed to get a fire up. Cuthbert inspected the flue, expecting to find a family of wintering finches lodged inside, such was the state of abandonment in the cabin, but it was clear. He was surprised, too, to find wood in the shed and not peat. He made a clean fire and then leaned back in a rocking chair waiting for dinnertime while Loeb searched the cabin for clues.

Loeb had imagined Cuthbert pipe in hand after a meal, caressing a round-bellied snifter, telling sad tales of defeat, but Cuthbert was a teetotaler and his teeth where white, so there was no hope of easing tensions in the cabin. Loeb himself had brought a bottle of single malt and a pack of Dunhills to the table. He lit a cigarette.

"You're a hunter," Loeb said.

"No, sir, I am not."

"I thought—"

"Why?"

"Because your brother said."

"I don't do anything," Cuthbert said.

"But you know the land."

"I know it."

"What do you mean you don't do anything?"

"I have no hobbies, sir. I sit. I don't drink when I sit, I don't smoke. I don't talk when I sit."

Loeb was uncomfortable being addressed this way by a man so many years older than him. He stood and said, "Isn't it odd that there's nothing here, Cuthbert? Not a single scrap of paper? Do you think he'll be back?"

"I told you what I think."

"That he's dead, yes. But let's assume for a moment that's he's not."

"Fine."

"If Lewis is not dead, where do you think he might be?" "Far from here."

"I see. Why? Because you noticed something about the ashes in the fireplace, I bet. You were able to determine the date of his departure?"

"No, sir, as far as I know you cannot do that." "What then?"

"It is my feeling."

Loeb sat, realizing his exhaustion. He saw that it was only half past seven. It felt much later, as if the marsh's thick darkness had also slowed down the passage of time. He said, "Should we search the area in the morning then?"

"You may, but I wouldn't advise it."

"I see. And why not? That's the first thing we learn to do in school, to make a visual map of the area under investigation." Cuthbert was silent.

Loeb said, "I said this is the way I was taught to work."

"He is not here," Cuthbert said finally. "If he is not here, it means he is somewhere else."

"Around here?" Loeb asked.

"You have missed my meaning."

"What then?"

"We should check Fleggsburgh. They will tell us there if your man has been through."

Loeb took his whiskey back to his bed to update his journal. Cuthbert sat, and as he had said, seemed perfectly content doing so. Loeb would have to ask him in the morning what he thought about while he sat.

Loeb watched Cuthbert feed the fire mechanically at intervals until he drifted off to sleep with that image in his mind's eye. What seemed no more than forty-five minutes later, he was awake, shivering under his goose down comforter. According to his watch, it was just shy of seven in the morning.

"Shall we set out then?" he called out to Cuthbert, who was still sitting at the table.

"We shall."

"Shall we eat first?"

"I've eaten," Cuthbert said. "Two hours ago. You may eat." He indicated the remains of a loaf of bread and a chunk of butter in wax paper impaled with a bread knife. Loeb got to his feet. The cold cut right through him. He debated sinking back into the goose down. Then he thought of dragging the blanket to the table, but imagined Cuthbert's disgust if he did. He hurried to his coat, dusting off his hat.

"Chilly," he said.

"It was your idea."

Cuthbert was paring his nails. Doing something, in other words, Loeb thought.

Loeb went to the pantry to see what Lewis had stocked for his expedition, realizing with some embarrassment that he should have done this as soon as they'd arrived. The condition of the pantry would tell them how long Lewis had intended to stay. Unfortunately, the light bulb wasn't working. He removed a jar and brought it back to the table. The lid said quince preserves. He was pleased with his discovery.

"I'd say he's alive."

"Oh, yes?" Cuthbert was grinning. Loeb was momentarily disoriented.

"Larder well stocked?" Cuthbert asked.

"Actually, it is. If a man brings along so many jars of this size, I'd imagine he plans to stay for at least a year. And I don't see what's so funny. Do you have a problem with jelly?"

"No," Cuthbert said, tapping the lid. "I have no problem with jelly."

The jar was filled with what seemed hundreds of tiny bird eyeballs in a dark, viscous pickling sauce.

***

Fleggsburgh was across the marsh on the old road. Cuthbert suggested they stop there for lunch and then head north, skirting the river, to Hunter's Yard. They could ford the Thume north of Ashby. The next day they would loop back around to Pilson Green, skirting the river on the east. Cuthbert knew people in Ashby who might have heard something. They drove in silence.

Loeb had packed a single book, Lockerson's classic, Along Elbow Creek. Lockerson had heard tales of the Calusa Indians collecting trophies from the birds they shot down and using them in their

rituals. The eye of the heron was supposed to make you see and shoot straighter. The Calusa chiefs would eat jay corneas before battles to give them aerial views. Nothing Lockerson had said would explain the jelly jar, however, or the other jars they'd found in the pantry.

Loeb noted in his journal that the macabre surprise in the cabin meant that something had indeed happened to Lewis and that only the man who had prepared the jars would know what that was.

It was a fact that Lewis's continued presence in the Broads might have stirred the resentment of local poachers. As Cuthbert himself had said, making a body disappear in that wilderness wouldn't have been difficult.

In Fleggsburgh they put in at The Prior's Rest. Their appearance attracted little attention from the locals. After a pleasant meal and pint of ale, Loeb inquired into Lewis's whereabouts.

The rosy-cheeked man behind the bar seemed not to understand. Loeb mentioned the ornithologist's business in the Broads and his disappearance from Pilson Green, the empty cabin. He said nothing of the pickled eyeballs. Still, the man claimed to have heard nothing.

"The man who collects bird sounds," Loeb said finally.

"Ah, the man who collects bird sounds," the bartender repeated for the whole pub to hear. "Why didn't you tell me? Lawrence?"

A very thin man in a tattered wool vest and cap stood with his ale.

"Ek, ek, ek," he said. "Ek, ek, ek."

"What is this?" Loeb asked the bartender.

"This is the man who makes bird sounds," the bartender said.

"But I told you we are looking for an ornithologist, not a man who makes bird sounds."

At this point Cuthbert stood, dissolving that union.

"Perhaps I was mistaken," Loeb said.

"Perhaps you are not," a small man in a corduroy suit whispered into Loeb's ear. He had appeared as suddenly and unexpectedly as Gough's collapsed wallpaper. Loeb waited for the man to speak.

"When the winter moon is full and the Broads bathed in silver moonlight," the small man said, "and the candle lights are all snuffed and even the bat will not fly from fright, a man in his cups must stick to the path."

He paused to lick his lips. Loeb was jotting furiously.

"For fear of the Bird Man! Ek ek ek!"

The whole pub erupted into laughter. Loeb sat and finished his ale. To his annoyance, he saw that it was barely half past three and Fleggsburgh was already sunk in gloom. They decided to stay until morning.

A dismal fog crept in overnight and Loeb woke trapped in its slow gray smoke. He checked the time and his watch face said just short of seven. Again, he had the feeling that he'd slept for no more than an hour. He was almost sure of it. Physically, he was exhausted. He closed his eyes, pulled the covers tight, and set into what he imagined would be an extra hour of badly needed sleep. But then he heard the Range Rover purring downstairs. He parted the curtain and there was Cuthbert perched neatly at the helm.

Loeb rushed into his clothes and coat and brushed his teeth. He ran downstairs and paid for the rooms. He would miss breakfast, he reflected on his way out the door, and he hadn't washed his face.

In the passenger seat moments later, Loeb said to Cuthbert, "Since I'm paying you for this, I'd appreciate it if we arranged departure times together."

"I believe we did," Cuthbert said.

Loeb turned to look at Cuthbert. Cuthbert kept his eyes on the road.

"I said seven o'clock and you agreed." "When?"

"Last night."

"I don't remember this."

"You were drinking."

"In the future I wish you'd at least wake me." "I can do this."

"Say a half hour before you're ready to pull out." Cuthbert nodded.

"I feel exhausted," Loeb said.

The fog didn't lift and Cuthbert grumbled about driving through it. But this was nothing compared to Loeb's disorientation. When the darkness lowered in Ashby, he could claim not to have seen the sun at all that day. He wondered if his watch needed winding, but when he checked the clock on the Range Rover's dashboard, it showed a difference of only three minutes.

"I feel like I'm not getting any sleep," Loeb said. "Is this possible?"

"You'll sleep in Ludham," Cuthbert said.

There had been no sign of Lewis that day, no cabins, shelters, lookouts. Minutes after they'd forded the Thume, Loeb had caught sight of what he thought was a lookout in the trees. He also saw a ragged form in the trees, gliding from branch to branch, a shape far too large even for a carrion bird. But Cuthbert, sitting by his side, had observed none of this. And then the sun was gone.

By five they'd finished their dinner at The Dog Inn in Ludham and Loeb went off to investigate. He was determined to be in bed by seven. Not wanting to make a fool out of himself at the pub, he walked the streets of Ludham.

As luck would have it, the first business he came to was a sporting goods store. The man behind the counter was pleasant and helpful, but he claimed to know Loeb, a patent absurdity. He said Loeb had been in not a week ago for some netting and flares.

"You mean Lewis," Loeb told the man.

"If that's your name, fine then. You never told me it. You needed flares for the poachers."

"Did I?"

Even if the man were mistaken, Loeb realized, this information could be useful.

"The poachers from Ludham or Ashby?" he asked.

"I don't believe you specified."

"Of course. And I told you I was doing what exactly?" "You should be careful, Mr. Lewis," the man said. "Loeb."

"There are men about who are none too happy to be spied on by Americans."

"But I'm British."

The man now wore a sullen expression.

"I mean Lewis is British," Loeb said, "who I am not." "Good evening, sir," the man said and he went back to his business.

Loeb finished his walk at the town square. The shop owners along the way had uniformly shooed him out of their shops. One man had actually pushed him out, blaming him for what seemed a family tragedy of some kind. A young boy in another shop had simply pointed and hissed.

Loeb circled the square and headed back to The Dog Inn, feeling bewildered. He knocked on Cuthbert's door. There was no answer.

He joined Caffrey, the innkeeper, at the pub downstairs.

The pub was empty, the fireplace long dead. Loeb ordered a half pint and sat at the bar hunched over its motionless amber surface, his thoughts wandering. In seconds he had fallen asleep that way.

"Your man has changed rooms," Caffrey said.

Loeb nearly toppled his beer with his forearm. "My man? Do you mean Cuthbert? He's changed rooms? But why?"

"He gave no reason."

"Where is everyone?"

"Home."

"But it's only— Tell me, Caffrey, what time do you have?"

The innkeeper shrugged at a plastic clock hanging over the cash register. The clock was stuck on midnight. How strange, Loeb thought, for a pub. He said, "But you must keep the time, to close up."

"The customer knows best," Caffrey said wearily.

"I suppose you don't have much of a problem anyway," Loeb said. "Did Cuthbert mention an Englishman named Lewis to you?"

"He did mention this name."

"And did he mention that I was looking for him? That this was the purpose of my visit?"

"I will tell you what I told your man," Caffrey said, "and it is this. There is no man by that name who has passed through Ludham. If there was such a man, he would have passed through my pub."

"But that's preposterous," Loeb said. "You can't claim to know every single person who has ever been through Ludham."

"Ever," Caffrey said.

"Even those who passed through before you were born?" Caffrey sipped his whiskey. He declined to comment.

"I see," Loeb said. "Well perhaps he went some other way—not through Ludham."

"Then I would know," Caffrey replied. "Perhaps he did not come this way after all." "I would still know."

"You would not know. How would you know if, for instance, he bypassed the Broads completely and sailed for Germany via the North Sea?"

"There is no man named Lewis," Caffrey said.

"No man?"

"He does not exist."

Wide awake now, but still groggy from lack of sleep, Lewis left fifty pence on the bar top and stood. For a moment he forgot where the staircase was, where he'd come from. Then it came to him.

On his way he turned, and caught Caffrey in the same position as he had left him, lifting his whiskey to his lips in what seemed exaggerated slowness.

Caffrey said, "We have changed your room too, Mr. Loeb." Loeb was already out of the pub when he heard this. "Changed my room?"

"As you asked."

"But this is impossible, obviously," Loeb said. "I'm perfectly happy with my room."

"Your new room, yes. I am speaking of the old room." Caffrey's words penetrated Loeb's tired brain in a haze.

"What do you mean, old room? How could there possibly be an old room when we arrived today, just this afternoon?"

Caffrey dropped heavily from his bar stool and slowly made his way behind the bar. He said, "Mr. Loeb, I am not in the habit of standing complete strangers to drinks, but in your case, it is warranted. You need this drink, Mr. Loeb. More than most you do. When you've finished, you should go up to your room. I will instruct the girl to let you sleep in, though your man would have you up at half six, according to your wishes."

At least he hadn't imagined his conversation with Cuthbert, Loeb thought. He sat and drank Caffrey's whiskey and then Caffrey gave him his new set of keys. He shuffled up to his room.

Had he really slept here for a night, at The Dog Inn, and forgotten? He decided it must have been his strange sleep condition that had played this peculiar trick on him. He settled into bed without taking off his clothes and shut his eyes and was engulfed by the most merciful of sleeps. And then he was awake.

Both Caffrey and Cuthbert were standing over Loeb, peering meaningfully into Loeb's heavy, clouded eyes. For a moment, Loeb couldn't respond. It was if he'd been buried underwater for millennia and then suddenly lifted out and forced to walk. His chest felt as compact as cement. He couldn't breathe. Cuthbert took his right arm, Caffrey his left. The two men helped him into his coat.

"I'm sorry, Mr. Loeb," Caffrey said, "but check-out time is twelve

sharp. In your case, I've made an exception, but the girl goes home at three."

"I—Is it that late already? Where is my watch?"

Loeb searched the bedside table frantically but it wasn't there. He was led downstairs by the men, and out the door and into the Range Rover. Cuthbert paid Caffrey from Loeb's wallet and then they were off.

Loeb formulated ideas, questions, as they drove, but couldn't articulate them. He wondered why if it was day the sun had already sunk, or was about to. But then he had a vague memory of similar sunless afternoons in the Broads.

Once he said to Cuthbert, "Via the North Sea." "Yes?" said Cuthbert.

"He may have escaped via the North Sea." "Who?"

"Our man."

"Caffrey?"

"No, no, the bird man."

"I have no idea what you're talking about, sir," Cuthbert said. Loeb's glazed eyes buzzed furiously in their sockets, as if they were cemented into that position against their will. "You don't?" "We should be in Pilson Green by dinnertime," Cuthbert said.

A memory at last!

"Yes," Loeb said, tears in his eyes. "And we will say hello to Mrs. Gough in the back room."

Cuthbert kept his eyes on the road. "Are you telling me that you've been through Pilson Green before? When we met, you said you had come from Great Yarmouth."

For a moment Loeb was silent. Then he said, "I feel sick. Please stop the car, Cuthbert."

A slanting drizzle had begun to fall, tossed about by sudden gusts of sour inland wind. Cuthbert could hardly see to pull over. They hadn't cleared the marshland yet and there was no sign of the road to Pilson Green. When they stopped, the tires lost traction and the Range Rover sprayed mud until Cuthbert drove up a grassy rise whose plateau was lost to the headlights. Loeb had already fallen asleep against the door.

"We are stopped," Cuthbert said.

"Yes," Loeb said, snapping to.

"Are you still sick?"

"I think it's passed, but I need to use the bathroom."

"Can't you hold it?"

"I'm afraid not."

"The wind is blowing. There is no visibility."
"I won't be long."
"You'll need this."

The flashlight was heavy and Loeb stumbled out into the mud with it. Cuthbert was right, however, the light worked against him, turning the needling raindrops into a hail of effervescent white sparks. Loeb moved his head this way and that to avoid them as he staggered after the flashlight's beam.

He stumbled on, to the top of the rise, and stood there looking down. Fifteen yards ahead a cabin with a smoking chimney caught his eye. He turned once more to verify the Range Rover's position, waved to Cuthbert and set off.

Descending, he noticed that it was no longer raining, or had stopped raining on this side of the hill. The temperature had risen and the saturated air had gathered. Through the swirling grayness Loeb could make out, like the green eye of a hurricane, the faintest smudge of sun. He left the flashlight on a rock and approached the cabin. He pounded wildly on the door.
"Lewis!"

Loeb continued to pound, and when there was no answer, he tried the door handle. The door fell open easily and he stood there for a moment on the threshold, searching the cabin for life. Inside, the fire had sunk to embers. Loeb quickly lifted his coat sleeve to cover his nostrils. In the corner of the cabin a ragged figure began to stir.

***

It was weeks before news of Loeb's disappearance reached Cotter. Cotter immediately sent a replacement named Daleworth to check up on Loeb. Morford had passed away that year but Budge was notified and directed Daleworth to Pilson Green, the last name Loeb had mentioned before leaving London.

Daleworth arrived the next day and put up at the Thume Hotel. He was encouraged to see that the guestbook showed Loeb's name, the date he'd arrived—November 22nd, 1973—and the date he'd left.

"Unfortunate," Gough said.

"You remember him?"

"Vaguely. An American."

"He was looking for a man named Lewis," Daleworth said. "He was being paid to write an article."

"I don't recall any of this."

"He stayed with you for two nights?"

"If that's what it says," Gough said. "He was on his way east. There's a man at the pub down the road who can tell you more. He can drive you anywhere you need to go. But perhaps you'd have a tea with me first?"

Daleworth didn't want tea, he wanted out of this dismal place and a flight back to Chicago, where his wife of six months was waiting for him on a sofa under a window that rattled with the El. A week out of journalism school and he'd already joined the endless ranks of hacks who ate their three meals at Mozel's, churning out copy no one read for the likes of Cotter. He wasn't getting paid nearly enough. He lifted his bag and set off for the stairs.

"I have something you may find interesting," Gough said.

"Later."

"Have you ever seen an armless and legless woman? My wife is both and she can light a cigarette using just her lips."

Daleworth dropped his bag and found his notepad. He joined Gough behind the curtain.

The End.

Case #71201

Max Sheridan

Max Sheridan lives and writes in Nicosia, Cyprus. He once hacked for the Cyprus Mail, a low-circulation newspaper—until he challenged the film critic, a notorious windbag, to a duel. His short stories have appeared or are forthcoming in Thuglit, DIAGRAM Magazine, Ampersand Review, Fried Chicken and Coffee, The Writing Disorder and Atticus Review. His latest novel, Montcrief, is seeking able and loving hands. You can find Max Sheridan here: www.maxsheridanlit.com.

CLAYTON HILL SANITARIUM

Justice Served

John Mc Caffrey

Physician: Dr. Peterson
S268-WCT29

DAN BENT OVER HIS WIFE AND DIPPED the spoon into the foul-smelling liquid in the glass. He spooned some into her mouth, holding her chin to keep her mouth closed. He tilted her head back forcing the liquid to seep down her throat. He noticed the color returning to her cheeks as well as movement behind her eyelids.

"Shel? Can you hear me?"

He lifted her chin, forcing more of the liquid to trickle down her throat until she began to cough lightly, then gagged and lurched forward in the chair.

His heart raced, but he kept his hand on her chin, "Swallow it Shelly."

Her eyes fluttered open, then rolled in her head as her chest heaved. She grimaced but did as he asked, then pushed his arm away from her and coughed loudly. When her coughing subsided, she slumped back in the chair, her breathing labored and ragged. Dan touched her wrist, feeling for a pulse. It was erratic, but as he held her hand, it steadied.

"Are you okay Shel?"

She nodded and pulled her arm away as another bout of coughing took her. He gently patted her on the back until the coughing passed. She slumped back in the chair; her eyelids fluttered as she gripped the arm-rests. Placing the glass on the end table he held her shoulder with one hand as she made a disgusted face at him.

"Shel, are you okay? Can you hear me?" "I think I'm going to puke," she croaked.

He felt relief wash over him and managed a smile. "No, you won't, and you have to drink the rest of it," he said as he stroked her hair. He gazed at her closely as she slumped in the chair. Her breathing was becoming steadier and the color was definitely back in her cheeks. He glanced at the clock on the wall noting the time; 12:02. He picked up the glass again, raising it to Shelly's lip.

"Drink this."

"No," she said pushing his arm away. She gripped the arm-rest tightly with her other hand as she surveyed the room. "Where are we? Who's house is this? And what the hell happened?"

Her eyes found his face as he held the glass close, still kneeling beside her.

"What happened? Did I pass out?"

Dan lifted the glass to her lips once again, "I'll explain everything later. For now, drink this."

"No, that stuff tastes like shit. Where are we Dan? How did I get here? What's going on?"

He sighed and reached for one of her hands, enveloping it in his own. While he was glad she didn't remember, he didn't know how much he should tell her at the moment. He decided less might be for the best, at least for now.

"You're sick baby. That's all. We were sitting in the living-room and you lost consciousness. You've been having spells lately, that's why you have to drink this. This will make you feel better. Okay?"

He glanced again at the wall clock; 12:05. "Please drink it Shelly, it's important." "I'm sick?"

"Shelly, please," he said raising his voice a bit. "Please just drink." She looked closely at his face, then down at the glass. She took it from his hand and raised it to her nose - sniffed it, grimaced - and drank it down in one swallow. The look that came over her face would've been comical if not for the situation Dan thought as he took the glass from her hand and set it down on the end table. She leaned back in the chair; her face screwed up into revulsion. He patted her hand and stroked her hair.

Her face looked as if she had just bitten into a lemon. She opened one eye and looked at him, "That is some nasty shit."

He smiled at her and glanced up at the clock, 12:09. He looked closely at her face. Even though she was grimacing, she looked good. He moved his hand to her wrist and could feel her pulse thrumming strongly. "How do you feel?"

"I feel like I just gargled with sour milk." "Seriously, how do you feel?"

"Cold," she said as she lifted a hand to her forehead, brushing a few strands of hair out of her eyes, "and stiff. I feel tired most of all, like I haven't slept in a week."

"Okay. You have to drink another in one hour," he said as he stood.

"Wait," Shelly said grabbing his hand. "Wait. What in the hell happened? Why did you say I'm sick? I don't remember getting sick. What's going on? Whose house is this? Tell me what the hell's going on."

"It's not important Shel. Just relax there for now. I'm going to rinse the glass. I'll be right back."

"No," she said raising her voice and gripping his hand tighter. "Tell me what's going on. I don't even know what day it is. Tell me goddammit. Why don't I remember? Please, you're scaring me."

He looked down at her, uncertain how to proceed. He didn't want to scare her more than she already was, but he also didn't want to tell her the truth just yet. Since every other attempt had failed, he was still dealing with his own shock. Until she opened her eyes and started talking, he wasn't certain it would work. He looked into her eyes, and although they were bloodshot, she seemed coherent and rationale. He decided to hold back the worst of it, at least for now, at least until dawn.

"What do you remember?" he asked as he knelt back down. She glanced towards the television, then her eyes wandered around the room as she spoke, "I remember going to work. I drove in because of the rain rather than take the train. I got off work and walked to my car..."

Her voice trailed off as she looked at him closely, then shook her head in frustration. "That's the last thing I remember. Was that yesterday? Did I have an accident after I got off work? Is that why I can't remember anything?"

"No, you didn't have an accident. You're sick is all, and I've been taking care of you. You'll be okay. You'll be fine now," he said as he stroked her hair. He glanced again at the clock, 12:16.

"Dan," she said in barely a whisper, gripping his hand with both of hers, "I'm scared. I don't recognize this room, or this house." She looked around, trying to take in everything. "The furnishings are ours, but the room is wrong. Where are we?"

She looked at him and reached a hand out, placing it on the side of his face, "Tell me please. What's going on? What in the hell happened? Why do I feel so cold and stiff? My joints ache and my head feels strange."

He reached a hand up and took her hand from his face and kissed her fingers, "Shel, don't worry about it for now. I'll tell you everything, I promise. Tomorrow. Okay? I'll tell you everything tomorrow. Let's just make it through the night. If we make it through the night then everything will be like it was. Trust me. I'm taking care of you."

He pulled her hand against his cheek and smiled at her. She returned his smile hesitantly and nodded. She opened her mouth to speak, but no words came out. She opened and closed her mouth a few more times then leaned back in the chair gasping.

"Hey," Dan said releasing her hand and grabbing her shoulders.

"Shelly? Shel? Are you okay? Talk to me," he shouted.

Her mouth continued to move but no words came out as her eyes rolled up into her head. She began to gag and suddenly pitched forward in the chair and bent over double, one hand going to her stomach.

He grabbed her as she began to slide from the chair. He called her name repeatedly as she slipped to the floor.

"What's happening to me?" she said, finally finding her voice. She moaned, still clutching her stomach as Dan knelt over her, holding her as best he could. She felt cold, and the color was slipping from her face, leaving her looking pallid. Her skin felt clammy as he grabbed her wrist, feeling for a pulse. It was growing weak.

"Oh, Shelly no," he whispered as he held her close.

Her eyes found his, then lost focus as she lie still on the floor. He drove his fist into the carpet, so close, so fucking close. He wiped at his eyes then scooped her up - her lifeless form already felt as if it were going stiff - and carried her to the couch. He clutched her to his chest and looked up at the clock; 12:21. He laid her down on the couch and straightened her white robe around her. He knelt down and closed her eyes, then sat on the floor with his dead wife, holding her hand. He lowered his head and cursed his own inadequacies. He'd read the material in the book numerous times and followed the instructions to the letter. Yet, he told himself, twenty-one minutes this time. That was the best he'd done so far. Progress of any sort was a good sign. He wiped his eyes and squeezed Shelly's hand once more then stood and retrieved the glass before walking to the kitchen. He flicked the lights on, and stood with the glass in hand staring around the room vacantly. He resisted the urge to throw the glass against the wall, and instead walked to the sink, rinsed it quickly, and set it down on the counter.

He crossed the kitchen to the cellar door, opened it, and peered into the darkness below. The flickering of the candles barely lit up the bottom of the stairs. He clicked on the single dangling light bulb that illuminated the descent, then went to the living room to gather his wife. He smoothed her hair, and whispered her name once before lifting her in his arms. He made his way down the cellar stairs, ignoring the two unconscious men strapped to the gurneys. He crossed the cement floor to lay Shelly down on the cot he kept next to the large reach-in refrigerator he'd purchased at a restaurant supply house. He opened it, and gently placed his wife inside, touching her cheek once before closing the door. He checked the thermostat on the refrigerator door, then turned to stare at the two men he had bound in the basement, his hands unconsciously clenching into fists. One had regained consciousness and noticing Dan, began a pathetic mewling from behind his gag.

"You want to shut up," Dan said quietly. "Trust me. You want to shut up."

The man lifted his head as far as his bindings allowed from the gurney, his eyes bulging and pleading, but he did as ordered. Dan crossed the basement and stood just outside the elaborate circular diagram he had drawn in the men's blood on the basement floor. He sighed deeply and began blowing out the black candles that stood in their sturdy metal holders around the circumference of the diagram. He needed to check his captive's restraints, but he didn't want to disturb the diagram on the floor just yet. He had to study his notes first. When she opened her eyes and actually spoke, he thought he had it this time, but something had gone wrong, in the end. He had to figure out what. He crossed the basement and turned on the overhead florescent, then sat at his desk.

He was certain he was getting closer; tonight's attempt was the best so far, she'd actually been coherent. He pored over his notes, checking and rechecking the diagram he'd drawn. He stood and compared the diagram drawn in the book to the one he'd made on the floor. It looked properly done, yet still the failure. Why? He sat back in the chair and ran his hands through his hair. He'd spent all their saving on the new house and on the books that lay scattered around his desk, and while the books held promise, he still wasn't able to figure out how to do the spell properly. The house had been a necessity, not only for the large basement he required, but also, he had to live in a place where he wasn't known. He needed privacy, no friends, family, or overly sympathetic neighbors stopping by. Tracking down and overpowering his two captives had been the easiest part of the whole task. Getting this spell to work properly however, was discouraging.

He glanced up at the newspaper clippings he'd taped to the wall in front of his desk. He made it a point to look at them every night, they helped him maintain his resolve. They preserved his focus on the task at hand, hardening his heart to what he had to do.
He wouldn't allow himself a modicum of sympathy for his two captives. They deserved their fate.

TWO MEN CAUGHT IN THE BRUTAL RAPE AND SLAYING OF SUBURBAN WIFE

He knew all the clippings by heart, having read them over more times than he cared to count. The montage on the wall was the brief history of the two animals bound to the gurneys behind him. There were black and white prints of their mugshots. Editorials of their troubled past and numerous dealings with the police throughout their pathetic lives. There was even one article where the mother of one of them had told the reporter what a good boy her son had been when he was younger. It was the last one in particular however, that he would read in its entirety before he went to bed every night. No exception. This one he had ingrained into his mind. The one that had made a mockery of the justice these two pigs so richly deserved. The one that had condemned them to his basement.

SHELLY BRENNAN KILLERS ACQUITTED ON LEGAL TECHNICALITY

He leaned forward and stared at the article. This one, more than any of the others, gave him the focus he needed. The accompanying photograph showed both of their smug smiling faces, flanked by their attorneys as they walked out of court that day. That most dreadful and shocking of days. He had stood in the back of the room as the judge had read his decision, and watched as the two pigs had shook hands with their attorneys. They had actually smiled at him as they passed by.
The bastards had smiled.
Well, they weren't smiling anymore.
Dan heard movement from behind him. The one who regained consciousness began his mewling again from behind his gag. Dan

looked over at him and their eyes met for a moment. It was now Dan that smiled and the animal on the gurney that looked away, pulling at his bindings. Dan turned back to his desk and opened the drawer that held Shelly's picture. It had been taken on a Sunday drive last year. They'd driven aimlessly through the middle of the cornbelt of Indiana. When they had pulled over and he took the picture, the sun had encased her in its amber glow, her hair seeming to float ethereally around her face. Her smile, deep and infectious, spread to her eyes that shone out the love she had for him. That had been such a nice day, just the two of them out for an easy drive. That had been one of the last truly wonderful days they had spent together. To have it all stolen by two sociopathic animals who escaped justice was too much for him to bear.

But now, justice had found them. Justice would be served. Now they would pay. Now they would pay with their lives to replace the one they'd taken. Now they would pay in blood.

He picked up his notes and looked them over once more. He'd drawn the diagram properly, using the blood of her murderers. He'd lit the candles in the proper sequential order and had recited the incantations correctly. The elixir had been painstakingly prepared and he'd started administering it to her at precisely midnight. She needed to drink one every hour until dawn for the spell to be permanent, but until tonight, he hadn't been able to keep her animated more than a moment. Tonight though, was a break through. Tonight, he had awoken her for twenty-one minutes. Tonight, he decided, had been a success. He jotted down the nights attempt in detail, then closed the notebook.

He rose from his chair and took the mop and bucket from the corner and washed away the diagram on the floor, then lined the candles along the walls for tomorrow night's attempt. After replacing the bucket, he checked the I.V. drip for both his captives. He needed them healthy until he was successful. They were both awake now, staring at him with pleading eyes.

He stood before them glaring, ignoring their plaintive whimpering.

"You'll both live long enough for this to work, and not a moment longer" he said looking at each of their faces in turn. "You'll pay for what you've done. You'll pay with your own blood, and when I'm finally successful, you'll then pay with your life essence so that which you killed can live again. You'll have to find forgiveness from
your maker when the time comes, because you won't be getting any from me."

Dan clicked the over-head florescent off, then crossed the basement floor and walked up the steps. He turned and shut off the light to the cellar stairs and closed the door to the darkness below as the two men strapped to the gurneys began screaming behind their gags.

The End.

Case #20086

John Mc Caffrey

John Mc Caffrey writes tales of horror, the supernatural, science fiction, and fantasy. He was born in Illinois and grew up on the south side of Chicago. While still in grade school, he developed a passion for reading through the works of Tolkien, Poe, and Lovecraft as well as being addicted to watching Hammer Film's at the local Saturday matinee. Today he lives in northern Indiana with his wife and two dogs where he writes in his spare time. His works can be found at Amazon, Barnes & Noble and Smashwords as well as various anthologies.

CLAYTON HILL SANITARIUM

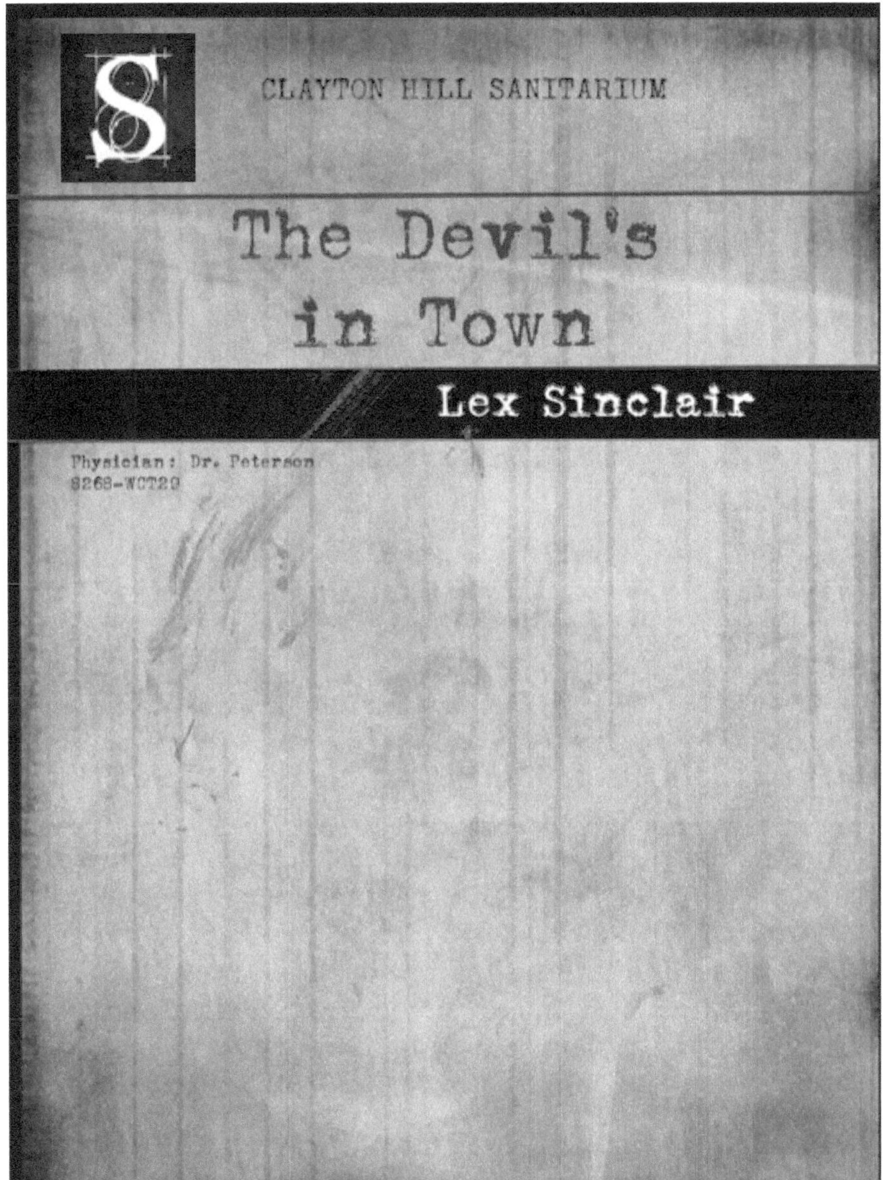
CLAYTON HILL SANITARIUM

The Devil's
in Town

Lex Sinclair

Physician: Dr. Peterson
S268-WCT2G

THE SUN SCORCHED THE VILLAGE IN SOUTH WALES in August 1994.

A man dressed in black strode along a deserted road after materialising from a crow leading to the nearest village. The dark man went by the name of Michael Embry. However, Michael wasn't the man's real name. He wasn't even a man. He was something far too sinister to have been born on earth.

Nevertheless, every one hundred years the malevolent dark man would descend the floating clouds and walk the earth to breed. Some would say that Michael Embry was the devil disguised as a man. He would roam the earth seeking out a female who would give birth to his offspring. His seed would be in the child, so that when the child was older, he or she would rule the earth. Hell wasn't beneath the earth; it was earth. Human beings were tempted by the devil every day to commit sinful acts. Michael pulled the lapels up around his neck as the wind picked up. He could see the village beyond the colourful mountains below.

The sun beamed down on the village through the sparse clouds. Dawn soon evolved into day, and the residents of the small town awoke, ready to enjoy the glorious sunshine on this Sunday.

***

Katie Reese got up earlier than usual this morning, having slept well the night before. Katie was eighteen and still a virgin. She lived with her mother and father in the suburbs surrounding the small town. Every Sunday morning Katie would attend the church service with her mother.

Once Katie and her mother got dressed, and had eaten a light breakfast they left for the morning service at the local church.

When Katie was younger, she didn't mind being dragged along to church with her mother every Sunday. The children went to Sunday school, where they could make pictures, drink squash, sing hymns, dance, and read. But now she was older, and no one else her age still went to church. She could be out in the back-yard sunbathing whilst reading a book or listening to music on her walkman instead.

It wouldn't make me any less holy, she thought.

Katie and her mother sat in the pews listening to the sermon read from the Bible by the Rector. After they had prayed, they were served the holy bread and wine. Once the Lord's Prayer was recited with the service was officially over.

Katie suppressed a sigh of relief. The mass of Christian believers departed the church to the outside.

Michael stood by the surrounding stone wall watching the congregation file out. He smiled, mocking the folks who greeted him jovially, shaking his head inwardly at how naïve they all were. His eyes widened when he saw Katie walking amidst the small crowd. Their eyes converged and he smiled at her. This time his smile was entirely genuine.

Katie was immediately attracted by the tall, handsome man gazing at her and pleasantly reciprocated his smile. Her stomach performed somersaults when she saw the tall, dark stranger approaching, ignoring the mass of townsfolk as they parted like the sea.

Katie stepped onto the pavement, forgetting her mother who was too busy gossiping with her friend to notice Michael nonchalantly sliding his hand up her daughter's skirt and groping her firm buttocks.

'Hello Katie. I've been looking for you, for a long time,' Michael whispered in a voice as soft as silk.

'How'd you know my name?' Katie's cheeks flushed a rosy pink. 'I know you. And I know you don't want to be here anymore than
I do, do you?' Michael smiled again and caressed her most sensitive area with delicate fingertips.

Katie shook her head, suppressing a gasp.

'Meet me here tonight at seven,' Michael said. 'You will be here won't you?

'Yes,' Katie heard herself gasp. 'I'll be here.' 'My name is Michael Embry'.

Katie couldn't fathom never mind articulate her emotions to this mysterious stranger. It wasn't like her to be so acquiescent. She was quite wary and coy when it came to the opposite sex. Yet Michael made her loins burn with a newfound vivacity and stimulation she'd never experienced until now.

Whatever it was – lust most likely, she thought – she couldn't get enough of it. She was hooked.

***

For the rest of the day that was all Katie could think about – meeting Michael at the church grounds at 7pm. She lay on top of her towel on the back lawn absorbing the sun-rays. Katie couldn't stop thinking how good it felt when Michael had touched, groped, explored her. Her father was cooking burgers and sausages on the barbecue, but food was the last thing on her mind. When the barbecue was done, Katie ate her food outside with her parents' not listening to a word of their conversation.

Once she had eaten, and the sun had slipped beneath the horizon, Katie went back inside the house and showered. She soaked her hair and body with the shampoo. Katie caressed her wet, soapy body all over, with trembling fingers thinking of Michael's hand touching her earlier that day. She envisioned him standing in the shower stall with her, groping her again, pressing himself against her.

After her warm arousing shower, Katie got dressed in her black nylon underwear and a white blouse. She used her most expensive perfume, before leaving the house on foot and making her journey to the local church with a spring in her step.

***

Michael was already sitting on the stone wall outside the church when Katie arrived. The two smiled simultaneously and then kissed passionately on the lips.

'I can't believe I'm doing this,' Katie said, voice quavering. 'Doing what?

Katie shrugged 'You know?' she said. 'Meeting up with someone I don't even know'.

'You do want to be here with me. Yes?' 'Yes. Of course.'

'Good. I want you to want to be with me,' Michael said.

Michael wrapped his arms around Katie and gazed into her eyes. She could feel him searching her soul. He made her feel like she was special. Like she were a goddess.

Michael guided her around the back of the church out of sight from passers-by then sat on the grass and watched the sun go down for another day.

Michael talked about how he felt about life, and how he didn't believe in God. Katie, who listened intently began to see things more clearly through his perspective and agreed. Michael's beliefs concurred with her conscience. He said that God was created by the human race, as a man in the clouds who looked down on earth and cared for every person like they were a child of his own; when in reality God cared about no one: that was why bad things happened to good people all the time. If God cared, then why didn't he help the ones he cared about?

Katie's grandmother had died of breast cancer a few years back. At the wake she had pondered the same things. She told Michael that she lost her faith when her grandmother - she hardly knew - died early in her life, and that she had cursed God for making her grandmother suffer.

'According to the Bible that is a sin,' Michael said. 'But if God has all these great powers and gives human beings their talents, then why does He take it off them so suddenly? And so painfully?'

Michael shook his head in disdain. He told Katie she was the same good person that she always was. Just because she didn't believe in God any more was irrelevant. It was then that Michael leaned closer kissed her on the lips, and rested his hand on her cheek. Katie enjoyed his kiss; his touch; the way it made her feel.

'You know what I want, don't you?' Michael whispered in her ear. 'Yes,' she said. 'I want you too.'

Michael slid his hands under Katie's blouse and caressed her breasts, feeling the nipples harden. Then he caressed the innocent girl between her parting thighs. The lovers removed their clothes until they were both naked. Michael manoeuvred himself on top of Katie. He smiled reassuringly at the girl before plunging deep inside her.

Katie screamed in pain: this was the most unbearable pain she had ever endured. Michael pinned her down using all his strength, until he was finished.

This isn't how it's supposed to be! her mind screamed.

When Michael had ejaculated inside of Katie, he rolled off her, uninterested.

But now it was too late. Katie's hair had instantly turned grey. Her life as she had known it ended right then. The true identity of who the tall, dark, mysterious stranger who went by the name of Michael Embry revealed itself all too late for her to undo her lustful

sin. She had the devil's seed inside of her. She would give birth to the Anti-Christ. Katie had subconsciously known that Michael was not human. Yet she had given in to her temptations and now paid the ultimate price. She mouthed the words of the Lord's Prayer that very morning, but hadn't listened to the meaning, now she wished she had.

Katie now knew who Michael was, and what he wanted from her. Her heart thudded hollowly, devastated. Michael's face was the same, but it had metamorphosed, and now she could see into his eyes - the eyes of the devil.

'Our child will change the face of this earth,' Michael said. 'And you and I shall stand side by side and support our child'.

Katie was speechless and still in shock at what she had done with him.

They got dressed just as it was getting dark.

Then, just as Katie was contemplating what she was going to tell her parents and how they would react to her being pregnant, Michael seized her arm in a cold, steel grip and took her with him. Katie knew then she would never be going home and that she would never ever see her parents again.

She belonged to the devil now - now and forever.

***

They checked in at the nearest hotel downtown and were put in the most luxurious room. Michael had no money. However, when he stared into the proprietor's eyes something unfathomable transpired. The proprietor succumbed to whatever he saw lurking in the chasm of Michael's eyes. Nothing more had been discussed in relation to Michael having no money. Instead the proprietor ordered the desk clerk to escort them to their room on the top floor.

Katie had not spoken a word since Michael had impregnated her. She sat on the edge of the double-bed and watched Michael open the door to the balcony.

He was satisfied that he had found Katie and seduced her. Now she was going to be the mother of his child, who would rule the world. He turned away from the balcony and glanced at Katie who hadn't moved from her position since they arrived. Michael had walked the earth many times before and created a son or a daughter, but they had failed to defeat the good people who still believed that God was great, and the creator of heaven and earth. The people of the world still believed in the power of good over the power of evil. The good outweighed the bad for now because the majority of people made the right choices - but that was going to change.

Michael believed that humans were imprudent beings who still lived in a world where no one was entirely free. The people still lived in a world of rules. Everyone that had done wrong was punished. Things like revenge were still a sin. Michael disagreed with the goodness in this world. They seemed to think they were perfect. However, there were some humans who were absent of morals, and did what they wanted to. Those people were the ones who were going to help change the world. The devil was cast out of heaven by God. Now God ruled both heaven and earth.

Soon the devil's son was going to give these people a choice to side with him.

Michael gazed up at the clear night sky and smiled. He knelt in front of Katie and took her hand. 'You done well, my love,' he said. 'You shall live forever in my kingdom of darkness, watching over our child as he walks into his destiny'.

Katie just stared at him, and then touched her grey strands. 'Look at my hair,' she said on the verge of tears. 'Look what you've done to me'.

Michael got to a vertical stance and kissed her lightly on the forehead. 'You'll be fine.'

The devil removed his coat and hung it on the back of the sofa, then took the phone off the hook. He crossed the room to the bedside cabinet took out the Holy Bible and carried it to the balcony and hurled it into the main road outside. Astoundingly, the tome struck a cyclist on the head. He lost his balance, swerved onto the wrong side of the road and slammed into the front of an oncoming bus, before being knocked down.

A woman screamed, turning heads and silencing the pedestrians and motorists going about their daily errands. The bus driver stamped on the brake, only it is too late as the wheels have already crushed the cyclist's dead body, mashing it into the concrete.

The cadaver emerged at the rear of the large vehicle twisted at impossible angles, unrecognisable, nothing more than a bloody pulp consisting of outstretched limbs.

Michael shrugged indifferently, pleased with himself for causing that to happen, by force of will.

Katie covered her face with her hands. Her eyes registered shock, but her whole face had collapsed with a profound melancholy. Then her head slumped forward and she began to sob. Michael walked in and rested his hand on her shoulder as she wept.

'There, there,' Michael said. 'As the Bible tells us – shit happens'.

'Oh, shut up!' she screamed.

Michael glared at Katie, eyes full of malice and considered throwing her over the balcony, but remained calm, only because she was carrying his child.

'People die every day,' he said, matter-of-factly. 'So, don't start crying and pretending to give a shit all of a sudden'.

'Murderer!' Katie barked.

Michael crossed the room where the television set was. He switched it on and flicked through the channels until he got bored. When he had looked up from the screen Michael could see that Katie had finally fallen to sleep. He wrapped the quilt over her and put his coat on before stepping out.

***

Michael roamed the streets looking for sinners to obey his commands. His appearance blended in with the environment. An old lady hobbling down the street in the opposite direction stopped suddenly after glancing into his eyes. She gasped. Then pointed her bony finger at him, but no words came out no matter how hard she tried. Michael had hushed her by putting his finger on his lips.

'He who walks among us,' she whispered.

Michael leaned towards the old lady and stared right into her eyes. 'You will die in your sleep, tonight Barbara,' he said, loud enough so Barbara could hear and no one else.

He walked on leaving Barbara standing motionless on the pavement, too frightened to look over her shoulder, and too afraid to go to sleep later that night.

Michael kept his head down as he strolled through the random streets. Some wise, religious freaks had the gift to see through his disguise and spot who he really was inside the body he wore.

His psychic powers informed him that Katie hadn't left the hotel, but that she would probably be up by now. He liked walking the earth alone; it gave him time with to think. However, he preferred

to fly in the disguise of a crow. It seemed more natural and less conspicuous.

***

Upon entering his hotel room, Michael instantly noticed that Katie was no longer lying on the bed where he had left her. He could feel the draught of wind in the room. The bathroom door was shut, but the balcony doors were wide open.

Michael approached the balcony and saw Katie standing on the edging looking down at the heavy flowing traffic below. She turned her head and faced the devil, tears brimming. She took immense pleasure in his expression as he stared at her unable to do anything if she jumped or fell from her precarious position.

'What are you doing?' Michael hissed.

'Do you feel vulnerable, Michael?' Katie asked.

He glared at her with malice, hands clenched into taut fists. 'This is what it feels like to be human, to be powerless,' she said. 'Get down!'

Katie shook her head, defiant. 'The power of good is far greater than the power of evil, Michael,' Katie said. 'I have sinned, just like every human being who has lived. But even though humans make mistakes – we are given the chance every day to learn from them and to make ourselves a better person. A holy person. I now know what must be done to save my soul'. 'That's nonsense, and you know it,' he snarled.

Katie ignored his statement 'You can't defeat the good in me,' she said 'The truth shall set me free.'

Michael lunged for her as Katie plunged over the balcony into gravity's inexorable grip. Then he watched as the mother of his child crashed through a car windscreen that had parked outside the hotel, killing both the child and herself instantly. Shattered glass twinkled under the hotel lights as crimson rivulets chased each other down the road to the gaping storm drain.

The seed was destroyed; there was no devil's child.

Not for now…

The End.

Case #32806

Lex Sinclair

Lex Sinclair was born in Wales, United Kingdom in 1983. He is the author of five horror/suspense novels such as, Nobody Goes There, The Lord of Darkness, Killer Spiders, The Goat's Head & the sequel Neighbourhood Watch. Some of his short stories have appeared in previous Sanitarium magazine issues, where he hopes to publish more. In 2010 his short story The Dies is Cast received Runners-Up Prize in the Terry Hetherington Young Writers Award. His poetry has appeared in anthologies and The South Wales Evening Post.

Also, his novels The One Eyed Monster, Abducted & I Wish have been earmarked for publication in the foreseeable future, along with the trilogy series Don't Fear The Reaper.

He currently resides in Skewen, Wales where he is busy working on his next writing project. He is proud to be part of Sanitarium issue 22.

All his novels are available on Amazon and other web sites.

CLAYTON HILL SANITARIUM

CLAYTON HILL SANITARIUM
Wendy's Promise
S.L Dixon
Physician: Dr. Peterson
S26S-WCT29

Long BEFORE SHE EVER HEARD THE PLEAS or moaning, she smelled him. His sweat, his piss, his shit, his bedsores, his smell revolted against her senses, but she kept a level head about it all.

They were her own words, the words that trapped her forever. Things were so different back then; times were different and people were different. Sure, lots of girls jump in the sack with any old boy and the first time she asked Isaac, she expected him to say whatever it took to get her to open her thighs. In reality, she just wanted to toy with him, she didn't know what she wanted from life, she was only sixteen and that was more than twenty years ago.

"Wendy," said the voice, so weak and ruined from the bedroom; he stretched the E sounds and held them, "Weeendeee, please," his voice hummed a reprise. Sometimes, she just had to ignore him.

She put the cans of creamed vegetables into the cupboard over the sink, next to the cans of soup and cans of meat. Everything was a puree; it was easier on Isaac's insides. "Weeendeee."

She closed her eyes and leaned against the sink, kicking her foot against the lower cupboard the one where she kept the drain cleaner, wire scrubbers and the garbage can. The idea was there again and it wasn't the first time. She just couldn't do it.

"Weeendeee, I so hungry. Weeendeee, I think I pooped again." Yeah, no doubt, he pooped, shit the goddamn bed, but he couldn't help it. It was thanks to that drunk; he crossed the line. The drunk was broke, drove without insurance and walked from the hospital into police custody with little more than a scratch while Isaac would never walk again, never gain full motion in his arms and never see life from a completely vertical angle. The stew of innards had to stay at a very particular angle or the tubes fell and the result of whichever bodily function from whichever tube found a home on the sheets.

He'd been moving again; she could smell it.

"Wendy, please."

For eighteen long years, it was always Wendy, please or Weeendeee, please, give or take the length of the vowel sound hold.

"Will you love me forever, no matter what? Will you love me even if I get fat and ugly? Will you love me even if I become a vegetable? Will you love me always?" she asked him over and over, it was a game, a game a thousand young lovebirds play, but a scare brought the question under a new and grim light.

It was the kind of thing that happened somewhere in the world, but never at home, never where you stood. Buildings collapse on the news and it was always so sad, but it never really scared you until you saw people scatter and the world come down.

Wendy and three friends drove south to a Barenaked Ladies concert in Toronto. It was great fun, but Wendy drank too much before the concert and needed some water on the way home. It was an especially snowy winter and the trip home took significantly longer than the trip down.

Looking back, she wished she'd noticed all the snow on the roof. Later reports suggested that the owner, a very recent immigrant from a snowless Asian patch of civilization, knew nothing about moving snow. He bought a building and opened a Becker's Milk, easy peasy, bring on the eighty-hour weeks and the fifty-grand a year income.

There was an inquest after the dust settled and the snow cleared. Wendy and her friend Becki went inside while Robin stayed out to keep the car warm. Wendy went for the fridge and Becki had to check her 649 ticket. Wendy had a habit for reaching to the back for everything: milk, bread, fruits, veggies and everything else, water included. She opened the windowed fridge door and leaned in to get a tall jug of clear gold from the back. That's when the ceiling creaked, she didn't hear it over the hum of the fridge's compressor, but Becki and Jim, real name Yun Geun-yong, stopped where they were and looked around. It was obviously a bad news kind of sound, but that's as far as either had a chance to think. The roof collapsed.

Becki and the man with Jim on his nametag both died. The sturdy frame of the fridge saved Wendy. She had a broken ankle and in comparison, that was like a cough in a leper colony.

The following morning Isaac got the call and raced beyond the road-closed signs and through the drifting banks. Wendy was fine, but she was all panic and little rationality.

"Promise me, promise me," she demanded, hand in hand with her long-term boyfriend, three years is a big deal, or was in the 90's.

"OK, I promise, babe. I'm just so happy you made it..." "OK, you promise what. I want you to say it."

"OK, I promise to love you forever, no matter what, even if you get fat, even if you become a vegetable. I will love you always, Wendy," said Isaac and he meant it so far as anyone could see.

They kissed and held each other for a long time. Three month later Wendy limped up the aisle in front of family and friends. Her father walked by her side, having a tougher go than she did. It was the last day she'd see him. He died the day Wendy and Isaac returned from their honeymoon in Mexico. It was a sad day, but he'd been sick ever since her mother died, it may not be logical or provable, but for some, heartbreak causes sickness. The cancer was pretty well everywhere in his body and where it wasn't, it had road maps ready and vacation time booked.

The promise became a regular thing, but it was fun again, the gravity ceased importance...

"Weeendeee."

until the accident. They'd had three glorious years wed underway to four and then forever. It was like a dream. Every day Isaac went off to brick homes, and schools and businesses while three and a half days a week Wendy answered the phone at the high school, they didn't give her full-time for financial reasons, she didn't see why she'd need extra insurance anyway. Every weekend they went somewhere new and special. Two nights a week Isaac and Wendy went out for burgers, or pizza or ice cream. It was perfect.

That one Friday morning changed everything. Phil Unger was out all night. He started the night eating ten-cent wings and drinking watered-down beer served by the jug. He bumped into an old school chum, Malcolm; they both dropped out of the tenth grade and took jobs their separate ways. Malcolm drove a forklift in the ice cream plant and Phil shovelled grain at the Co-Op mill, both had Friday off and neither saw a reason to call it a night when the bartender stopped serving them.

Malcolm lived just a few concessions over and explained his stash of primo coke, so long as Phil knew some primo honeys. The coke wasn't primo, but neither were the honeys. They snorted and danced the night away, both picking their honey (one man's ditch-pig is another man's honey and don't you forget it) for the night. It was a sloppy and blubbery go and thanks to the coke, the plumbing on both sides refused cooperation.

Phil left a little after five in the morning with a limp noodle, full nuts and a hazy gaze from the drinking and snorting. He weaved to and fro over the yellow line on the empty highway, driving thirty kilometers beyond his turn before he realized and turned back around.

Isaac kissed his sleeping wife's forehead before he took his lunch pail out to his truck and headed toward the site. The local bigwig masonry company fell behind on work for the new hospital and in order to keep the second half of the contract, they had to meet every time constraint. Killhammer Construction, the company who whom Isaac worked, stepped in to claim the enticing opportunity. Isaac made it thirteen kilometers from his home, nine kilometers from where he stopped to grab a coffee and six kilometers from the work site when he met Phil Unger on the highway. Considering the little things, the things that could've changed an outcome along a timeline always offer a bounty of possibilities that don't end in an accident, but thinking about it could drive anyone insane.

"Weeendeee, I'm so hungry. Weendeee," Isaac moaned helplessly. "You promised, Weeendeee."

The accident was so long ago, the last time she spoke the promise, even longer. She couldn't do it anymore. Tears flowed and she decided it was time, but not the drain cleaner, that was cruelty,
to both of them, she couldn't do that. When her father died, she inherited everything he had, it all stayed in a storage unit out of town and she knew he had guns, he loved his guns, but they were illegal and the government won't kick a stink about something they don't know about. She kept those guns and on her way home from the grocery store, she stopped at the storage locker.

It was cold and heavy in her palm. When she was just a girl, her father showed her how to load it, showed her how to fire. She walked toward the moan and the stink, the gun behind her back.

The door creaked open and every time she looked at his pale white skin littered with bedsores and sickly veins, she saw herself, the years she'd spent watching over her husband, watching time suck the vitality from her skin; she saw herself in it all.
"Weeendeee."

She stepped closer, the smell bringing about more tears. She wanted to cover her face and run, but it was time, "I'm sorry Isaac, I can't do it anymore," she lifted the gun.

"Weeendeee, you promised, Weeendeee, pleeease. I love you Weeendeee," he said, three weak tears sprouting from his dry sockets. He attempted to lift his arms and fight her, but it had been so long since he could do anything but lay there, aging into a mass of open sores with anti-bacterial cream covers. "Weeendee, I looove yooou. Weeendeee."

"I'm so sorry, Isaac. I love you too," she planted the gun against his forehead.

"Weeendeee, you promised, Weeen..." his voice went no further and the pistol rang out.

She squeezed over and over, "I know, I know," she said as she unloaded eight shots into her husband's head. Looking down at the mess made it all real and she backed away. She slammed the door and continued backing away, dropping the gun to the floor as she hit the kitchen table.

"Weeendeee," she heard, it was light but it was there. She tugged at her hair, pulling bunches out by the roots.

"No, no, no, you're dead," she pleaded; the gun had to do it. She'd tried everything else. After the first few weeks of him home, she tried a pillow on his face, but it only knocked him out.

"Weeendeee."

She promised herself she wouldn't try again; he would go on his own time. She promised him. Five years later, he still hadn't gone and he'd drained her body and soul right along with his, she fed him rat poison. There was silence for three days and then...

"Weeendeee."

Those three days he didn't speak were utter hell; she still needed him and didn't know it, so when he did finally call she was happy.

"Weeendeee."

Over the years, she sliced his wrists, fed him drain cleaner and tied a rope around his throat, but he wouldn't go. She knew the gun would do it, but he was still alive. She promised and since the gun didn't work, she'd live up to the promise.

"Weeendeee," Isaac called out again and again until she answered.

"Hold your horses, baby. I'm coming," she started the blender and dumped in some veggies, cranberries and a quarter can of Spam. "JUST A MINUTE," she yelled over the blender's roar.

The Hornbeck family owned the bungalow next door and knew nothing of their neighbors, but when Royce heard those shots, he became mighty curious in a hurry. He dialed the police and since it was a small town they gave him the run around about how it wasn't likely gunshots, fire crackers maybe and if it was gunshots, it was probably a hunter outside town somewhere. Royce was adamant and thirteen minutes (there was a best of thirty-one Rock, Paper, Scissors game to decide who got to go) later a cruiser pulled into Wendy and Isaac's driveway.

Wendy heard the knocked on the door and stopped feeding Isaac the puree, "I think we have a visitor."
"I hope I'm decent enough to entertain," joked Isaac.

"You have an excuse, what about me?" Wendy asked, running her hands down a grubby apron over faded jeans and a faded sweater. She threw off the apron and raced to the door and before she left the room, she sprayed Lysol into the air; it promised to kill the bacteria, not just mask the smell.

She opened the door and it was a surprise to see two massive men on her porch, "Can I help you?" she asked.

One of the officers looked past Wendy and saw the pistol on the floor. It was his first good action in months and her pulled the paper-light woman from the doorway and threw her onto the grass.
"What the hell, Bobby?"

Bobby looked to his partner, "Check out the piece, Oggy." Oggy, given name Augustus, looked through the door and saw the gun. He entered and checked the kitchen, living room and bathroom before he came to the closed door at the end of the hallway.

From the ground Wendy recalled the gun and recalled its illegal status, she'd watched enough Law and Order to know to keep her mouth shut, so that's what she did.

Oggy raced back to the doorway, "Bobby, you gotta see this shit." Bobby smiled despite Oggy's sickly appearance. Oggy pointed

toward the room at the end of the hall and put one hand on Wendy's shoulder.

With the bedroom door open the scent flooded onto everything, even outside the smell was almost unbearable. Bobby covered his nose and continued. From the doorway, he saw what appeared to be the rotting outline of a body, covered in rotting baby food and anti-bacterial cream. He fought a retch and tore back to the outside. "You take her in and I'll watch the door. Call in everybody, that shit is fucked," said Bobby.

Oggy nodded and Wendy finally felt the urge to speak, "Who'll

watch Isaac? I promised him, you know?"

The End.

Case #85586

S.L Dixon

More of S.L Dixon's work can be found on his website www.SLDIXON.ca

Dark Verse

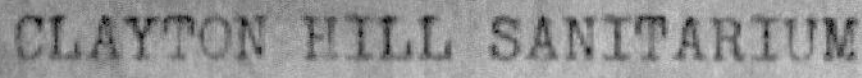

Physician: Dr. Salam
7128-DV758JJ

Kyle Short
Kanishka Narayan
Cecilia Dockins

Trapped in a fight, Forgiveness vs. Sin
The light cannot shine if you won't let it in
A world full of grief, decay and demise
A hollowing soul emits pain in your eyes

Your family and friends have all left you again
A life of despair to which there is no end
A darkness is coming, a terrible storm
Yet, without the rain we cannot be reborn

With mortar and stone you proceed with a wall
The lightning that strikes will not let you stand tall
With Innocent's death there is nothing else left
A pile of bones is where you choose to rest

An urn holds the ashes of what used to be
A bracelet of chains will not let you run free
You feel no one cares as you write your last will
(A beautiful flower can grow in landfill)

Wondering what your life has become
Instead of a hand, you pick up a gun
With agony piling on top of your head
"My family will be better off when I'm dead."
Such foolish a statement, words that are not true What in the
world will your family now do?
Your children will lead the same life that you have You're
taking your life and you're taking their dad

The smile you give to the ones who look up
To you, to the sky; they're the ones you'll corrupt How can you
be so selfish to act?
Do you still believe they don't care if you crack?

You'll leave them, disease them, throw dirt in their face
You gave them a home now you'll give empty space
A memory beaten and tired and torn
What will they do when they step on a thorn?

Who will tell them there is beauty to find?
Who will help shape their small, delicate mind?
If you choose to leave then you choose to deceive
A lie is the last trick you have up your sleeve

Put down the gun and step into the rain
The night is what prepares us all for the day
Look in the eyes of the ones who you love
They are the answer to prayer from above

Case #27617

Kyle Short

J Kyle Short has been writing for over seventeen years, only recently taking a serious turn at attempts to become published. He writes somewhat darker poetry that speaks about life and his personal viewpoint on the current standings of society. Albeit "dark" writings, there will always be a source of light trying to peer through into the eyes of the readers or characters involved. His mostly true stories have sparked an interest in persons going through struggles who are unable of finding help or seeing hope. J Kyle will continue to write as long as others will find use of his words.

Upcoming works include a self-publication titled A Poet's Blight which tells tales of struggle through rhyme. The everyday occurrences that afflict society are illustrated in these writings. A plague of drugs, death and dis-ease continues to sweep across the Nation; it matters not what race, creed or title an individual holds. In these verses the author attempts to show the Light that exists within the darkest, most decrepit of corners. In disparaging times, one must change their viewpoint in order to see the beauty that surrounds. We all may feel lost, yet we all are able to be found.

Welcome to the brink of Eden, Enjoy the soot filled air,
All are philosophical lepers here, men broken beyond repair.
No celestial beauty to see, no infernal punishment here,
All eyes are shut with indifference; in thick slumber we're all
smeared.

All truths have been forgotten, we have no time for lies,
We're seated at the walls of Eden, but the garden to us is
denied.
We live in damp lifelessness, wondering how time flies,
Wondering what mystical realm, beyond this high wall lies.

In the dreamlike state of solitude, our present turns to past,
We pray for an apocalypse, Let this moment be our last.
Welcome to the brink of Eden, Enjoy the soot filled air,
All are philosophical lepers here, children in despair.

END

Case #78485

Kanishka Narayan

Details not released
at this time.

At two a.m. I wake
cold, sweating, alone
lungs quaking at the sound of a howl in the darkened field
below. A solitary shadow passes my window,
moon shone.

There are things that go bump in the night
in the closet, in the wood, under the bed, in the heart.
And I come to the curtain to call, to peek, to seek the dark meat,
to chew on its bones
in the somber hours before the bright.
Between the shadows of the oaks and the turbid fog I notice a
glint of teeth, of fur,
a cocky smile, an inescapable lure.

The click of the lock is
overwhelmed by the scream of the rusty window undone as I
cry out to the Devil come, take me.

Case #44490

Cecilia Dockins

Cecilia Dockins lives just a bucket kick from Nashville, Tennessee. She spends most of her time wrangling words, kids, and pets. She doesn't like to bake and has a healthy mistrust of ribbon dancers. She does enjoy hoarding pulps and butchering flowers, which she describes as "gardening."

She earned her B.A. in English from Middle Tennessee State University in 2010. She will be a student in the upcoming Odyssey Writing Workshop this June. Her dark fiction has appeared in various anthologies. Look for more of her poetry in the forthcoming Horror Writers Association Poetry Showcase e-chapbook.

You can visit her at www.ceciliadockins.com

Or befriend her on Facebook: https://www.facebook.com/ccdockins

CLAYTON HILL SANITARIUM

Can you describe what your workspace is like?

I've got a stark work environment at home. I have a black Ikea desk. It sits in front of a big window with a big, cushy leather chair. I do about half of my work there. But there are several restaurants where I like to hang out, steal a table for a couple of hours, and write. Something about the random noise of strangers and people moving about makes it easy for me to slip off into my own world and get into a story. The weird thing about that is that I'm an introvert. I have a terrible tendency to avoid people, and I especially hate talking to people on the phone. But being among them in an anonymous fashion seems to work for me.

Do you have a go-to gadget / app or service that you cannot live without?

Whatever device I'm using to listen to music. I LOVE good music. *Do you have a set routine while you work?*

I guess I kind of talked about that on question one. I grab my laptop, get out of my cube at work, and run off to someplace noisy to write during lunch. I try to write at least 1,500 words per day, though if I'm really getting excited about what I'm writing, I'll pop out 3,000-5,000 words before I know it. But 1,500 is the minimum. I try not to let myself go below that. However, there are days, many days, during the book production process, when I'll be editing and proofreading instead of writing.

What is the best piece of advice you have ever received?

Don't be a pussy. It really is the foundational truth upon which all other advice is based. Take "be persistent," for example. All that really means is don't quit. Why do you quit? Because it's hard. Why is it hard? Because you're being a pussy. How about "treat others as you want to be treated'? What does that really mean? Don't treat them badly. Why do you treat others badly? Because you're afraid of something about them, or about yourself. Because you're being a pussy. "Speak softly and carry a big stick" is pretty much a paraphrase of "Don't be a pussy." "Don't be afraid to chase your dreams." ...You see where this is going.

Don't be a pussy.

Do you have a final piece of advice for our readers?

I always get to a point with everything I've written when I think it's total crap. Sometimes that's the first time I re-read it. Sometimes that day comes a few years later. The important thing is that I don't keep polishing the same turd, hoping to put an attractive gloss on it (at least, not anymore). Now, I work with something through five or six edits. If I get to the point where I like it, I publish it. If not, I save it on the hard drive and get started on the next work. The next one is always better, always.

The thing is, a turd will only get so shiny. The next turd in line will always shine more.

By the way, I burned my first novel and destroyed the soft copies. I have another completed novel on my hard drive that I'll probably never publish. I have a novel that I self-published and then pulled down when I couldn't overcome the feeling that it was complete shit. But I didn't quit writing (well, I did, several times, but I kept picking it back up and starting again). I kept at it and I kept getting better. You will too. And if you persist, and your writing improves to the point where you're happy with it, you'll be able to give your mom an autographed copy of your book, and random people will contact you online to offer you oral sex. Possibly even people of the gender you prefer.

A Little About Bobby:

There really isn't that much to tell. I'm pretty average in pretty much every way imaginable. I'm of average height. I have average colored hair and eyes. I live in an average neighborhood and always have. I had two kids and I have a couple of dogs. Like most folks, I sit in a cube all day and do work that I loathe for people who see me as a deleteable number on a spreadsheet. I've been in my current job two years and had three bosses. I've met each one in person once. I just love corporate America (apply sarcasm here).

School was always ridiculously easy for me, and I spent most of my time there being bored and daydreaming about other things (kind of like how work is for me nowadays). I was an excellent student, though I tried my best to be invisible. At work, I'm still trying to be invisible.

I trudged through most of my adult life putting in just enough effort to get by, because I always had this dream to one day be a writer, a dream I was always afraid to chase. It was always a one-day sort of thing. Well, my kids are in college or graduated now and I've worked a lot of years in jobs I'd rather not have been doing. And the truth about the advice question is that I heard it a long, long, long time ago, but I never believed in myself enough to take it.

Do what you love and you'll be successful.

It sounds like bullshit, but most advice does. At least it does to me. But I finally put a real effort into writing, doing what I love. And to my surprise, it's working out. I still have my day job, but in the last two months, my royalties have exceeded the pay I get from my day job. Maybe by the end of the year, I'll go full-time as a writer.

http://www.bobbyadair.com

Hello horror lover.
If you've been suffering from a persistent desire
for just a little more unpleasantness in your life,
we have the answer:

NOCTURNAL
TRANSMISSIONS

NOCTURNAL
TRANSMISSIONS

PODCAST

Nocturnal Transmissions is a fortnightly podcast featuring
inspired performances of dark tales both old and new
by voice artist Kristin Holland.

Find them at
nocturnaltransmissions.com.au
or wherever good podcasts are purveyed.

If you have any feedback or would like to leave a review please head over to Amazon and share your thoughts about Sanitarium.

Thank you for your time and we salute your love for all things horror.